395

Myself and Marco Polo

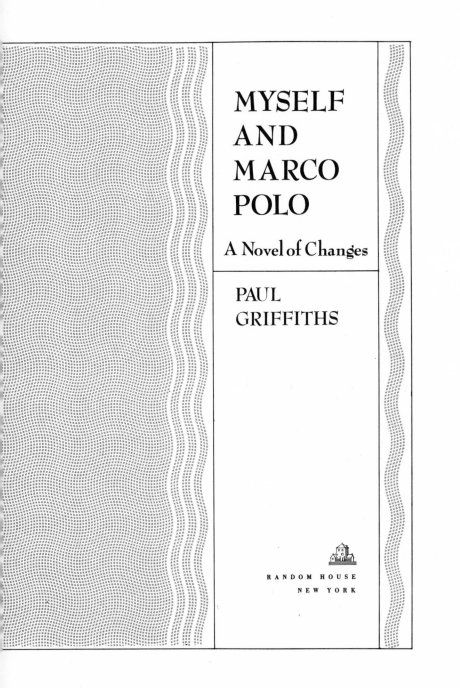

MYSELF AND MARCO POLO

POLO

A Novel of Changes

PAUL
GRIFFITHS

RANDOM HOUSE
NEW YORK

Library of Congress Cataloging-in-Publication Data
Griffiths, Paul.
Myself and Marco Polo / Paul Griffiths.
p. cm.   ISBN 0-394-58296-9
1. Polo, Marco, 1254-1323?—Fiction.   I. Title.
PS3557.R48945M97   1990   813'.54—dc20
89-10791   CIP

Manufactured in the United States of America
98765432
First American Edition

Book design by J. K. Lambert

for Rachel
and my Guangzhou brother

Myself and Marco Polo

I

in which I meet the famed traveler

You must know this isn't my métier: I mean the sea. We Pisans lean rather toward the land. This book too, among others. However, the story, such as it is, such as it was, began at sea, and so must I.

A voice returns, the first of many, or perhaps you'll say the second: "Venice *is* the sea, and only intermittently the land. You would do well, sir, before proceeding very much further with your narrative, to get your feet wet." My patron; the client for the Venetian romance on which I was newly engaged; and indirectly the instigator of this present endeavor. He does well to appear so early, and better to depart so soon, having pitched me into his gilded galleon, and so into the sea battle at Curzola on that 6 of September in the year 1298 (the facts, always the facts), and so here.

Let me explain. I was led from the quay by night, a hand on my shoulder and a rope at my waist, in a group with some Venetian notables whose clothing suggested the prospect of ransom: no doubt my patron's fur-lined cape had got me membership of this company. Of course, I entertained no hope that the undisguisable Pisan silt in my voice would bring me preferential treatment: do I need say that to be Pisan in Genoa is almost worse than to be Venetian? And indeed on that first night I was treated with the same blank unconcern as the rest. We entered a labyrinth of damp, low, flat-roofed corridors, with torches at intervals that accentuated the gloom more than they gave light. It might've been a cave, or a cellar, or a warehouse near the water. I couldn't tell, though now, since the days here are marked by some intrusion of weak gray light but not by any sound of an outer world, a cellar seems most probable.

That night I was in no condition to judge. Without warning I was firmly pushed into the room where I now sit; the door clanked with iron and wood behind. There was someone else in the room before me: a standing shape without feature, since behind him there was a candle on a sideboard, so that the outline of his back was framed in glimmering yellow, outshining the detail within. He turned, and the dark shape revolved without any element of the face becoming clear to me, except the prominent nose at a moment of profile. I did see, however, bunched in his right hand, a bundle of sticks: I was to see much more of those sticks, those fifty splints he fingers even now, during the coming weeks (and let those still to come be only weeks, not months, not years). And I was to hear other strange words than those he spoke softly as he turned: "The creative principle: sublime" (and here the lips meet at that "m" while in profile) "success." But then facing me his tone changed, and he spoke as if beginning again for public hearing.

"A sorry night for a meeting. My name is—" But you will

know. Here was the celebrated traveler, "il milione" as they say, the one I'd never hoped to glimpse in Venice, so surrounded was he by protectors, the importer of emeralds, fine Syrian dishes and yellow silks, the journeyer through half the world trapped with me within a few square yards of Genoese limestone. I couldn't have been more surprised if he'd declared himself to be the Archangel Gabriel, but I hope I didn't discommode him by showing as much. I quickly introduced myself, or rather reintroduced myself, for under very different circumstances, when Marco Polo was still a name and not yet a fable, we'd met at Acre. It was twenty-seven years ago. The Polos were being blessed on their way by the long-patient Tedaldo Visconti, suddenly become, after three years of cardinalatial wrangling, His Holiness Pope Gregory X. Of course, I was just an onlooker at that particular tableau, but I shook hands with them, the two leathered travelers and their apprentice, Marco, eighteen, still a boy. I never expected to see any of them again this side of damnation. But here I was, as yet undamned.

Don't imagine I expected him to remember that earlier touching of our paths. I could ask him even now, but I'd prefer not to. For one thing, I'm not convinced his memory is altogether reliable, and I certainly don't want to have to listen to his stumbling efforts to piece together what he thinks I want to hear—not when I'm personally involved, you understand. Anyway, he didn't clasp me around the neck and cry out: "Rustichello, my old friend!" No, none of that. We just sat down, as if the places at the bare wooden table had been prepared for such an action, with no sound as we took our chairs, except for the scrape of oak legs on flagstones. Then he put his hands on the table, fingers loosely interlaced, and looked me straight in the eye. "Well," he said, "what do you want to know?" That was all. As if after three years back in Christendom he'd got used to its being his part to spin tales of strange cities and perverse customs, of fierce Turks and luxurious Indians, of khans and houris, of battles and trades, and walls rippling over mountains, as much and whatever his hearer wanted.

(Is that how it was? You must know I'm already long past the beginning of this business, at a stage when it seems necessary to try to recall how and why it started. Notes, memoranda, diagrams, stories, explanations, queries fall about me. The task of collating them all looms depressingly. Some, of course, can be ignored.)

II

in which I make a proposal

Perhaps my first mistake was to introduce the suggestion of wonders. Slowly he leaned further forward, extending his forearms toward me and driving one fist into the other palm, while his face tightened in similar measure.

"I am forty-five years old," he said. "Twenty-four of those years I spent in Asia. It is Europe that is the stranger to me, in inviting me to understand what I cannot explain, in requiring me always to make sense of *its* wonders. I see a thin white pastry converted into the very body of my God, and yet it remains the same. I see Christ's praise of poverty spoken from golden altars to a pleased audience of senators in furs and cottons whose prices I know from my own exchange receipts. I see children begging in the arcades of San Marco, watched by the mosaic images of the one who claimed them as his own. I see a pauper's body floating facedown in the canal, bobbing like shit as it stirs in the wake from a bishop's barge. I see the one true Catholic and Apostolic Church a bed of squabbling infants, while the Holy Roman Empire has become a prize for German princelings. These are your wonders, sir, the themes for your epic."

The accusations of any adolescent. "God's mysteries," I said piously, "are beyond our understanding, and even further beyond my prose."

"In verse, then? A cento of cantos, perhaps. Would that be enough for your—" But his last two words were lost as the door banged open and someone else came into the room.

III

in which my work begins

It was, however, only a sharp-nosed, thin-faced, red-capped ser-
vitor bringing a plate of crusts and a jug of bilge, then leaving
without a word, looking as if he were thinking of something else,
indeed as if he belonged somewhere else. He's become a regular
abstracted visitant. This first time, after he'd gone, my new
companion sighed, as if to clear away our earlier interchange.
Perhaps the arrival of the refreshment, such as it was, had
reminded him that this wasn't going to be a brief meeting.

"I am sorry," he said. "It has been a long day, and a bewilder-
ing one. After avoiding capture by Uzbek bandits and Tartar
warriors, Javanese headhunters and Singhalese pirates" (I begin
to doubt we spoke so often in lists) "I find myself a prisoner of
the Genoese, a people apparently so little different from myself.

An hour here has perhaps affected me more than a quarter of a century in the East."

"I pressed too soon," said I. "We will talk more of these things tomorrow."

And so we did, after, at least on my part, a sound night's sleep on the pallets the Genoese had provided for us. We awoke. We tugged at more of the bread and gulped at more of the water. We said very little, but laughed in the way of men whom twelve hours of imprisonment have made into allies: perhaps travel could be similarly binding. We took it in turns to squat on a rattling iron bucket and to ignore the stench. We thought, perhaps, about how we might return to the easy communication that at first had seemed possible, and that so quickly had been lost from our grasp, without either one of us (so I believe) wishing it. We sat again at the table. We waited for him to begin.

"So, Rustichello, I am to be the figure for your next romance."

Care was needed. "As I intimated last night," I said, "out of your unrivaled knowledge of the world you could surely finish material for an entire library. And if we can persuade our dumb captors to give us the use of pen and paper, then I'd be more than happy to act as your secretary." (A nice word, I knew as I chose it.) "We may well, after all, be in need of some diversion." (And another.)

"What sort of a book do you have in mind?"

This was almost too easy. "It's more a question," I said, "of what sort of a book lies hidden in *your* mind. Is it a volume of travels and voyages, steering its words through the safe passages of far seas and mountain ranges? Is it a history of Genghis Khan and the Tartar lords?—a subject of the intensest interest to the reading public, I need hardly point out, when already the invaders have cast their scarlet cloak as near us as the plains of the Hungarians." (I embroider my words a little, of course. You wouldn't expect anything less.) "Is it a compilation of stories, or an anthology of legends, or a gazeteer of distant cities and peoples, or a description of natural curiosities? Is it a manual for the Far East trade, providing a judicious account of values and manufactories, routes and markets, such as might benefit a merchant in searching out the choicest cinnamon, the most profitable porcelain, the finest of the crimson carpets of Armenia?" (All these, I have to admit, the finger of my mind leafed through in some excitement. I could've written them all, with or without Signor Polo. But I didn't. Or rather, I won't.)

"I am not a literary man," he said. "Books are as alien to me as the palaces of my native Venice: I may survey the façades, but I do not see inside." He settled back into his chair, and I felt him slipping away from me again, beyond anything either of us could do to stop him (though I like to think I've since developed techniques, principally of antagonism, to keep his mind on the subject), as he continued: "You must remember we had taken very few books with us: a New Testament, a psalter, orders for Mass for our daily use, for baptism when we reached Cathay, for the burial of the dead should the occasion arise. All these I soon knew by heart: there was no need to read them. And though I gained a fair knowledge of several of the languages of the East—Tartar, Persian, Turkish, Chinese—their alphabets proved intractable. I could not read their histories, their bestiaries, their astronomies, their almanacs, their holy books." He looked down as I began to wonder at what those eyes had touched but not seized. "Or not much." And he raised his eyes again to mine. "My point is simply that I do not think in books, as you do. I cannot turn through my life as through pages, or see it stacked before me as a range of folios." (Of course, at this point I didn't realize how much his objections might be ironical, made for his own, or someone else's, amusement. He hadn't yet told me his stories of the Library of Unknowing, the Theater of

Irrelevance, the Guardians of Knowledge, the Game of God, and the Breaker of Categories.)

"Then it will be your part only to talk," I said. "The writing and the arranging can safely be left to me." (Did I really feel so confident?) And before we lapsed again into the numb hostility of the previous evening, before he could register any more doubts, I rose quickly and went to the door. I took hold of the latch and shook it as noisily as I could: it sounded like a dozen carts rolling past in that vacant corridor. I called out.

"Hey! Paper, ink, a pen!"

IV

in which the book begins

In Acre that plum and primrose dawn we found a Greek packet-steamer that could take us to Ayas. We gave it a rough tour of inspection, and though the accommodation it offered was something less than kingly, we were now in too much of a hurry to quibble with Fate when with a shrug she held out to us three gray bunks in a greasy hole. And I suppose we felt we might as well learn to cope with a degree of discomfort at the outset. After all, this was going to be a long jaunt. Dad and Uncle Maff had done the trip before, of course. They had also made some efforts to establish what could be useful contacts all along the route to Peking. But they had taken a different route out. Also, we knew a little too much about the precarious state of Central Asian politics to feel much confidence that the same people would now be in the same positions even of minor local power. Besides, because these journeys took so long, by the time we got to China it would be near on ten years since Dad and Uncle Maff had left Peking. We wanted to get on with the job. So we booked our passage with the Greek.

The trip, our last over water until we reached Shanghai, passed without incident, probably because Dad and Uncle Maff took it in turns to sleep. Given the opportunity, our amiable bushy-bearded Greek would have sliced his smile into our throats and consigned our bodies to the deep, our souls to oblivion and our gold to his pockets. We took a course only a few miles off the Palestinian and Syrian coasts, so that we kept on our right a thin view of the great Asian land mass, across practically the whole of which we were going to travel. It was a token, and a challenge. As for the sea, that was, as ever, the sea.

And so we came to Ayas: the northeast hole on the snooker table of the Mediterranean, and the sink of the Middle East. It was a haunt of Jewish moneylenders and Turkish brothel-keepers, Genoese merchants and Egyptian pederasts, murderous Syrians and Armenian peasants who came in from the surrounding countryside to filch and cheat. Every nation was represented by its lowest type, and as our boat came into the harbor, so a crowd began to gather at the quayside, like ants scenting sugar. For me it was a revelation. Acre had been very much a European town, sedate and gentle-tempered for all the heat of its streets. It was no longer a frontier post but a proper metropolis, with colleges, churches, hospitals. But now suddenly here in Ayas was the real Asia.

However, Dad and Uncle Maff were not a bit put out by all the bustle, the eyes, the red-checkered headdress on a man holding up documents of some kind, the gaze of a child who with untoward calm held forward a tray of oranges, the shadows of waving arms that played over other waving arms. They paid our grinning captain in the Nicaraguan silver dollars that are the preferred currency in these parts, then marched me (N.B. and the monks?) down and through the mill. Like Moses through the waters, we strode on firmly, and screens of bodies folded back on either side. But then there was a face Uncle Maff recognized.

"Ahmed Ibn-Bizna!" he exclaimed, and they fell on each other's necks in the prescribed manner. All the rest, realizing that here were old Levant hands and not gullible newcomers, melted away. Then, holding his grasp on the old Arab's shoulders, Uncle Maff stared into his tiny brilliant eyes, whose wetness seemed to reflect a genuine pleasure in the meeting.

"Ahmed, friend of my youth, Christ be praised Allah has spared you!" I was later to learn how useful this macaronic greeting was, maintaining as it did a decent dignity on both sides. The Ibn-Bizna, as Dad and Uncle Maff had told me long before, had done them great service when they had passed through Ayas on their return from China: lodged them in his house and secured them a safe passage back to Acre. The obvious question now was whether he could render us similar aid at the start of our journey in the opposite direction. We were, of course, too small a party to think of traveling alone. We would have to get ourselves fixed up with a larger outfit making for Mosul or Baghdad, or if we were lucky, going as far as Isfahan— though even that was a small enough step on the trek we were contemplating. However, to have discussed business with the Ibn-Bizna at this stage would have been a gross impropriety. First there must be the courtesies of invitations decorously extended, amazedly received, modestly declined, gently repeated and joyfully accepted.

It was not until the same evening, over a dinner of honeyed lamb among the trickling stone basins, curving ferns and lime-encrusted pillars of the Ibn-Bizna's courtyard, that the subject of his possible assistance was broached. And of course it was broached by him.

"Your lordships have surely not traveled so far once more merely for the pleasure of soiling your feet with the filth of Ayas," he said, with only the barest hint of the interrogative. Dad and Uncle Maff assured him that the great happiness of re-encountering an old acquaintance extinguished all other thoughts, as the sun extinguishes the stars. I was a little surprised at finding them tolerably good at this heavily complimented conversation. I saw them in a new light. But I was expecting they would then go on to say what our real reasons were for being in this God-awful stew of a town. I wasn't yet used to the hints and vacillations, about three levels beneath the actual conversation, by which business is transacted anywhere east of Cyprus. Of course I later learned how negotiations have to become ever more deeply buried and subterfuged the further east you go. Discussion in Europe is a great highway signposted by facts and outspoken opinions; in Ayas it was already a meandering lane; by the time we got to China it would be a footpath untrodden for a decade, barely distinguishable and certainly unmarked by sign or symbol. One travels into obscurity.

But I digress. The meal went on at its own pace. Daughters and sons of the Ibn-Bizna appeared from time to time with new dishes, new chimes in the gastronomic harmony. There were immoderately green vegetables floating in a turmeric sauce, flat balloons of bread covered with seeds, raffia tubs of nuts and figs and apricots, a paste of millet and orange juice, a salad of vermilion rose petals, a dish of sorreled eggs. The conversation continued too with its own flavors. The fact of our journey was, like the lamb, the main theme. The difference was that whereas the meat was grandly displayed on a rosewood podium in the center of the table, the matter of our traveling needs had to have a totally hidden prominence. The game—and I was by now a bit less astonished that it was played with quite as much skill by Dad and Uncle Maff as by the Ibn-Bizna—was to introduce subsidiary themes that were not overt denials of the unspoken subject, nor tracks away from it, nor yet attempts to lead toward it. To venture too close would have been presumptuous, of course, while to go too far off would have been discourteous to the host, whom both sides knew must eventually strike to the main question himself. He did so quite abruptly, as if the correct interval had just passed.

"If there should be any way in which a humble merchant of Ayas might be able to assist the noble signors as it has been his honor to do in the past, it would not cease until his dying day to be a source of joy and satisfaction to him." The words were spoken quickly and quietly, while the Ibn-Bizna's eyes were fixed without concentration on the lamb. The appropriate phrase in the ritual was being voiced, the permission for informality. Unnoticeably the daughters and sons had drifted through and beyond the colonnades, leaving us alone. Uncle Maff put down the silver cup that had been at his lips, and the chink resounded from the wet stone around.

"You will remember, Ahmed my brother, that when we were last in your company we promised we would return?"

"Indeed."

"Promised a promise we had already promised, many months and three thousand miles before, to the Great Khan himself?"

"I remember well, and rejoice that your promise, to me at least, should so speedily have been redeemed."

"Not so speedily, friend Ahmed," said Uncle Maff. "Two years and more have passed while we waited for the go-ahead from our blessed bureaucracy. But here we are. When we last met, you greeted us at the end of a journey. Now you bid us adieu at a beginning."

"And will endeavor to send you on your way in hope and health and assurance of safety," the Arab declared. "You will wish to join a caravan to Baghdad, to Isfahan? You will be taking ship from Hormuz, or traveling over land?"

"Our journey is not so well planned." Uncle Maff had some difficulty in avoiding the suspicion of stiffness, or worse, of hiding something. He coughed a little, and his wirebrush eyebrows arched as if they were independently animate and registering surprise. The trouble was that he didn't want to indicate to another merchant just how much our itinerary might be made flexible to accommodate commercial opportunities as they presented themselves. Of course the goal was set: Peking. And I had no doubt that Dad and Uncle Maff knew pretty well how we were going to get there. But a wandering trader has to leave room for himself to wander. "However, in the first place we would of course be looking to reach Baghdad as soon as possible."

Baghdad! The sound of the word was enough to have my mind swimming with images of the orient. The "b" was a broad white dome with a nipple turret, surrounded by four minarets, all harshly white except where the dust-brown smoke from vendors' braziers wafted. The "a" was the arch of a palm tree close by the eastern gate, where camel trains from Samarkand might pass through the high city wall, the shadows of trunk and fronds falling on them as they went. The "gh" was the gloom of a carpeted saloon, where naked women lay letting pearls drop through their hands while eunuchs came with copper trays of sweetmeats. And the rest was the distillate of nutmeg, myrrh and coriander in my nostrils, the azure of glazed tiles around a cusped doorway, the damp warm touch of a secret finger.

"You are fortunate," said the Ibn-Bizna, "and so am I that I can so readily afford you some small service. In three days my second son will be leaving Ayas to do business in Bukhara." He went on to insist that nothing would gratify him more than that we should accompany Emraz Ibn-Ahmed. Uncle Maff's demurs had to be murmurous so as not to offend, but no limits were set to his expressions of gratitude, and he took full advantage.

Even so quickly the conversation had slipped back into formal gear. We had said what we wanted; the Ibn-Bizna had offered a solution; the rest was a garland of courtesies. The daughters and sons reappeared with bowls of rosewater, strips of steaming linen, trays of salted pistachios and all the other accouterments to the ending of a soirée in the Persianized Arab style of this quarter. Then they withdrew to settle themselves in a whispering chain along the wall opposite where I was sitting, the swish of their confidences a cool cascade behind the sturdier voices of the Ibn-Bizna and Uncle Maff. I strained to hear them, and even so soon was touched by the sadness of the stranger. Here was a chattering group composed of my contemporaries, but through ignorance of their language I could feel no fellowship with any of them.

Except for one. Except for one delightful creature who kept herself somewhat aloof from the rest, even though she was sitting, or rather kneeling, in the middle of them. Her eyes strayed toward mine, and I eagerly accepted and returned their interest. But whenever our gazes met, she would snatch her head away, and her lips would quiver with what could have been either a forming smile or a muttered admonition. She was

dressed in citron silk—the whole company appeared to have
been got up to show off the Ibn-Bizna's merchandise—and her
black hair was bound with beads of turquoise, pearl, lapis lazuli
and red glass. And was there some other mineral color brighten-
ing her mobile lips and treacherous green eyes?

V

in which he intervenes

"No." Just that, the simple negative, dispassionate. He put down the sheaf of papers on the table. There weren't so very many of them at that stage.

"No what?" I said.

"It won't do. It's not the way it was."

"No, it's the way it is."

"But it's all fabrication. It's not the way I told it."

There was a pause. Perhaps he sighed before he leaned toward me and continued.

"I am but a poor merchant and traveler, as you know. But to me it seems clear that if something is so, then we speak truth in saying or writing that it is so. And if it is not so, and yet we say that it is, then we lie. And there's an end." I think I report him not unfairly, and thought it best to appeal to you.

"Do you imagine," I said, "that our readers will expect truth? Or will they look rather for plausibility?"

He was silent: is that plausible?

"Then with your permission," I said, and gathered up the papers from the table, "I will return to our work."

"Our work?" he said.

"The book," I said.

"The book is yours," he said.

"The book is its own."

VI

in which there is another

interruption

Listen. In the minds of three jade-carvers there is a single thought: I it must be to realize my ideas in the great piece of Burma stone that has been presented to our lord. The three carvers pressed him with claims, papered him with designs, thrust before him models of wax and clay: gryphons, lacework spheres within spheres within spheres, pagodas, coelacanths, puzzling mazes. But the lord could not decide among so many plans put forward all at once, and he knew, from an ancient precedent, that any threat to divide the block of jade would find goodness, not truth. And so he ordained that the carver should be chosen by chance, by the simple method of picking a short straw, and that then one of the other carvers should have the opportunity to beautify the efforts of the first, followed finally by the last to add his own embellishment. That way, he reasoned, the eventual carving would unite the best skills of all three carvers. He wondered whether to announce the full details of his scheme or to let the carvers know only that one of them was to be given the honor by the divination of randomness. He decided, and it amused him, to intrigue them with the whole plan.

So the first carver was chosen, and went away to his studio with the lump of stone. A month later he returned, and with some ceremony revealed a fantastic tree growing from within a butt ornamented with goldfish and waterlilies. The bark of the tree was intricately grooved; the leaves were finely figured with veins; and there were a hundred pear-shaped fruits hanging from the branches. More than that, attached to the tree by the slenderest spindles were twenty birds, each one different, all in graceful attitudes of flight. The lord was astonished, and all his court with him. Everyone agreed that no further beautification of the piece was possible, but the second carver, chosen because she was the eldest, took it away to her studio.

Once again the court assembled a month later to see the result, and once again the sculpture was borne in under a cover of tan silk troubled with roses. But this time there was a sound of the most complex tintinnabulation, and some of the courtiers guessed correctly what the second carver had done: she had converted each of the tree's fruits into a tiny bell, so that the tree rang as it stood, rang with an exquisite irregularity, responding with its miniature janglings to a footfall in an upper chamber or the thrashed air of a passing mandarin's robes. Everyone agreed that the piece had become the acme of delight and perfection, but the third carver, chosen because he was the youngest, took it away to his studio.

Again the court reassembled after a month, and again the sculpture was unveiled. But now no difference could be seen or heard. The lord frowned. The young carver, however, asked his attendants to carry the piece out into the garden, and the court followed. Once the jade tree was outside, there was heard from it a warbling and a whistling, a fluttering of glissandos in a music of constant variety against the thrill of the pears' chiming. Some of the courtiers guessed correctly (perhaps they would have been the same ones who had guessed before) what the third carver had done: he had drilled each of the birds in a different manner, making them work as an ensemble of tiny pipes, a symphony of wind instruments. Everyone gasped and oohed with the tree organ, and there was a shuffling of polite silk-gloved applause. Now it seemed indeed that the absolute limits of beauty had been reached, but at this point the first carver appeared before the lord and insisted on his right to work on the jade again. He pointed out that the second and third carvers had both started from something that had already been achieved, largely by him, whereas he had been obliged to begin only with what nature had provided. The lord agreed that this was just, and gave him leave to take the jade away again to his studio, which he did.

Once more the court gathered in the great hall of the palace after a month had passed, but this time there was no proud entry, no silk of tan and roses, no tantalizing shape or sound. After a while those present began to turn in whispers to one another, though some of the courtiers guessed correctly (perhaps they would have been the same ones who had guessed before) what the first carver had done, and with slow noddings they dispatched their servants to his studio. And with slow noddings those servants returned. The lord was informed of what had happened, and silently the court moved off to the place where the first carver had been found. There he was, on the floor of his studio, surrounded by fragments of jade that caught dull sunlight like shifty eyes, in his hand a green dagger he had made from the trunk of the tree, and on the dagger, scarlet on green, his blood. Many of the court turned their heads from the sight.

None wept: they felt too much the shame of what had resulted from the pursuit of beauty. There was silence, and loud thinking. But then the second carver spoke, and demanded of the lord the right to work on the jade again. She pointed out that the first carver had been given two chances, whereas she had received only one. The lord asked her to reconsider, asked her to dwell for a moment on the terrible thing that had happened. But she was adamant, and the lord agreed that her cause was just; he gave her leave to take the jade away again to her studio, which she did.

Then again the lord and his court came together a month later, much more somberly than on the four occasions before. Heads were cast down. No one wanted to meet another's glance. No one expected any sculpture to be borne in. No one began to get restless: everyone wished that the period of waiting might continue forever, that they might never be made to know what this fifth attempt had brought. For all of the courtiers guessed correctly what the second carver had done, though only some of them (perhaps they would have been the same ones who had guessed before) guessed the means. With slow noddings they dispatched their servants to her studio, and with slow noddings those servants returned. The lord was informed of what had happened, and silently the court moved off to the place where the second carver had been found. There she was, on the floor of her studio, surrounded by fragments of jade that caught the dull sunlight like shifty eyes, in her hand nothing, but at her mouth a trickle of crimson. Many of the court turned their heads from the sight, but the lord's doctors came forward to make an examination, and then to extract with their implements the jade plug, patterned with letters in an alphabet no one could understand, the jade plug which the second carver had made from the handle of the dagger and then swallowed. No one wept: they felt too much the shame of what had resulted from the pursuit of beauty. There was silence, and loud thinking. But then the third carver spoke, and demanded of the lord the right to work on the jade again. He did not feel there would be any need to repeat the argument that had been used by the second carver, and he was right. Nor did the lord think it would be useful to repeat his attempts at dissuasion, and he was right too. Instead he gave the sole remaining carver leave to take the jade away again to his studio, which he did.

Then for the last time, and they knew that it would be the last time, the court after a month reassembled. Still more somber was the atmosphere, still further cast down the heads. No one wanted to meet another's glance. No one expected any sculpture to be borne in. No one began to get restless: everyone wished that the period of waiting might continue forever, that they might never be made to know what this sixth attempt had brought. Yet none of the courtiers guessed correctly what the third carver had done, though some of them (perhaps they would have been the same ones who had guessed before) were quite confident in their incorrectness. With slow noddings they dispatched their servants to his studio, and with unexpected gestures those servants returned. Their masters were astonished. The lord was informed of what had happened, and in high hubbub the court moved off to the place where the third carver had been found. There he was, on the floor of his studio, surrounded by fragments of jade that caught dull sunlight like shifty eyes, though now there were many fewer of them, only enough to offer targets as smilingly he sat and rolled at them a small, perfect ball.

VII

in which the book continues

Possibly there was, but I was in no mind to care. Our eyes
danced together and ducked away until—and how many times
have I kicked myself for this since?—I fell sound asleep under
the influence of a repleteness I had not known since Europe.
Needless to say, the Ibn-Bizna would countenance nothing
stronger than sherbets of coconut milk and orange-flower water
at his table, but it had been many days since I had tasted
anything much beyond rye bread and stale beer. I had eaten
greedily, and now slept greedily. I had no recollection even of
the stumble to our room.

The next morning we slept till late, none of us stirring until
the sun had risen into the high vertical slit of a window in the
white wall of our apartment. Uncle Maff fussed about, saying we

had lost valuable time; Dad calmly ignored him. I began to understand why they could face a second long journey together. After all, there was no commercial sense in these endless expeditions back and forth across Asia, for profits that could never equal what one of our cousins could clear in a single afternoon on the exchange. Perhaps the escape from ordinary responsibility was, for both of them, an important part of the point. Uncle Maff, layer of grand plans, made sure that things were never normal; Dad made sure they were at least tolerable, which on that particular day meant making a tour of merchants, banks, brokers and agents.

Ayas was the last town of any size we would encounter before Mardin, a couple of hundred miles or so ahead, roughly halfway to Mosul. We therefore had to equip ourselves for a journey of several days. But more importantly, we were now at the very limits of the umbrella provided for us by Polo credit. From this point we would have to have with us sufficient gold, currency and merchandisable items to provide for our travels. Medical supplies, too, would be uncertain further east. If we were going to cope with Persian gutrot and sprains in the high Pamir, we would have to get the necessaries here. The whole journey had to be in our minds almost before it had begun. We had to know where we were going. Uncle Maff had some reason for his irritability.

The second evening at the Ibn-Bizna's was spent very much as the first had been, again with the Dancing Green Eyes in attendance. But there was an interruption. A boy in white trousers flashed across the torchlit courtyard to where the Ibn-Bizna was sitting peaceably discussing business with Dad and Uncle Maff over a basket of figs and sweet tea. His news was urgent and unexpected. Egyptian forces had penetrated the border and were already poised on the outskirts of the city. Within hours Ayas might be sealed under siege.

Gasps of fear and amazement on all sides. However, the Ibn-Bizna, bless him, was thoroughly in control. The caravan must depart forthwith, under cover of darkness, taking the northern route out of the city, through a gate which would almost certainly be the last the Egyptians could take. Emraz was dispatched to round up his men. Dad and Uncle Maff were interrogated about their state of readiness, congratulated on having concluded all important business, and urged to pack our belongings for a departure in two hours' time. We at once sped off toward our room, followed by our two young fathers, Nicholas and William, who so far had been keeping their heads down.

VIII

in which I pause

Of necessity, because they raise rather a problem. You see, if the religious aspect of the return visit to China was so important, why did the Polos begin their journey toward Peking before the election of a pope who could send the blessings the Chinese emperor expected? If it wasn't important, why did they wait two years before setting off back? If it was important, why did they leave Acre in the first place with only the commendation of the legate Tedaldo? If it wasn't important, why did they turn back from Ayas the first time to receive a benediction from him as the new pope? If it was important, why did they carry on after these two priests had deserted them in Ayas, given that they could easily have returned to Acre for other friars? If it wasn't important, why make this great journey back to Europe and so back to China at all? If it was important, why continue back to Peking and so risk the emperor's displeasure?

Is it merely sentimental to look for a motivation? Maybe. Did he go only to find himself in these pages?

We decided (after those first two nights in this prison we had started to achieve the first person plural) on a change of tack. He got out those sticks again, and after much shuffling of them pronounced: "The lesser nourisher. Success!"

IX

in which the book begins again

And it was one of those days when it seems much too rough a
word to speak of the dawn as breaking, because it is a slow
unfolding, like a flower, and there is no moment when you can
say that it happens, as you might say that a glass breaks. There
is no beginning to the dawning, and really no ending either, and
yet who would say that the dawn continues to midday, or to the
evening, or to the night, or to the next dawn? The ending is
simply irrelevant, because dawn is all about beginning, and it
occurred to me then that this journey, though it seemed now to
be beginning, really had started before, and that this departure
from Layas was only a further stage in a journey that had begun
in Acre, or in Venice, and that journeys are like dawns in having
no beginning or ending but only the continuing. And I looked

at the sky, where it appeared that long slender fingers of light gold and purplish gray were parting the air between them, but with no boundary between the fingers, only a fuzziness. And then I thought that the sky really is all fuzziness, and that the shapes we see in it are momentary and illusory, because I looked again and the fingers had gone, and there was just a line of tangerine a little way above the horizon.

All this, of course, was in the direction ahead. As had been arranged, we had stepped out of the city by darkness, and found waiting for us outside the northern gate, breath steaming yellow in the light of a lantern, a dozen horses for ourselves and those who were to travel with us, and six oxcarts covered with linen awnings, five of them filled with our baggage, which at this stage included our clothing, our money and some supplies that would serve both as emergency rations and as gifts for nomadic chieftains along the way: some dried fruit, and a few battered wooden cases of muscatel, and several boxes of fine biscuits we had picked up in Istanbul. Someone, too, had loaded us with drugs and bandages.

So we had left Ayas, and were now perhaps a mile beyond the city, not traveling at any great speed, because we were limited by the slow rolling of the oxcarts, but had chosen them for their sturdiness and reliability, and for the fact that we would not have to change the beasts, as we would have had to change waggon-drawing horses, at every night's staging. The oxen dragged at their own rate, while we, horsed, jittered about them, like flies about a purposefully swimming animal, making the same overall pace but pulling forward and backward, sometimes ahead to spy out the next stretch of terrain, sometimes behind to keep watch over the whole caravan, or else to glance back at what we were leaving behind.

And I think it was the wind in my hair that made me look back to the city (a kite hovered), and because I had been training my eyes on the sky ahead, now suffused with a color one might have called quite equally yellow or green or blue, because of that, I suppose, it was the sky that took my attention as I looked back to the west and saw dense clouds blowing toward us, promising rain, but not yet. And below the clouds, below the gray and rounded and quick-changing shapes, there was the stillness of the city, now beginning to catch the brilliance of the day, and to make a little light of its own. It was just at that point, if indeed it is a point, where a two-dimensional black outline is changing, through an increase of illumination, into a three-dimensional image.

And the only sound was the sound of birds, and the sound of men and women that was like the sound of birds in being an answer to the dawn, formal and necessary, so that this dawn chorus included as of right, without any dissonance or contest, the wailings of two or three muezzins from their minarets, which were just beginning to gain some of their whiteness against the dark green wool of the further trees on the Mediterranean shore, and included too the regular clang of the solitary bell in the tower of St. Stephen's Church, where I had stood in a squeezed congregation the Sunday before, and which I could not now see, because it was squeezed itself behind the fort, but which I could both see and feel in my mind, in arches and a basalt plaque and a quality of air summoned by the tolling of the bell. And it seemed that everything was well, as often it will at the beginning of the day, in the dawn, before the light turns up the noise of our aloneness.

X

in which he introduces Peking

You must know that for three months of the year, December, January and February, the Great Khan lives in the capital city of Cathay, whose name is Khan-balik. In this city he has his great palace, which I will now describe to you.

The palace is completely surrounded by a square wall, each side of which is a mile in length, so that the whole circuit is four miles. It is a bulkily built wall, and fully ten paces in height, plastered in red and battlemented. And it is all of the palace that most of the inhabitants of the city ever see: only those above a certain level in the mandarinate, or belonging to the khan's family or household, or serving at high rank in his armies, or venturing, as we were, from far beyond his realm, or about to go to their deaths at the place of execution, are permitted to see within. As I say, the palace is contained within a square wall, though from inside one might say that the wall is round, for its corners are hidden by its many separate buildings and stands of trees. Once one has passed through the gates, too, what is outside ceases to be of much consequence, partly because the wall shuts out sight of it, partly because there is so much splendor within. From the outside the walls impose for what they withhold; from the inside they are insignificant. One has entered a whole city of palaces and gardens, and wants no other.

At the northeast of this city there lies the rudest but, as I once heard the khan say it was to him, the dearest section: a little field of coarse grass about fifty yards across, a miniature wasteland seeming the more derelict for the fine houses that survey it and the carefully weeded walks that are its approaches. Yet this wasteland is in fact cultivated with the greatest assiduity. Every three years the soil is removed and replenished from hundreds of oxcarts that have carried earth from beyond the Great Wall. And every winter the khan himself takes off his silk robes to don the harsh sheepskin coat of a Mongolian herdsman, and then to sow, unshod, the bare plot with the seeds of prairie grasses gathered from far in the north. If questioned about this unswerving custom he might speak thus:

"When I was born, my grandfather Genghis had already long before fought and rode his way from the chiefdom of an insignificant clan to the governorship of half the world. My family lived and died in the saddle, or else under canvas, while gradually they learned more comfortable delights at the easy courts of Baghdad and Samarkand. Meanwhile our homeland lay empty, as still it lies empty; we have poured ourselves from it, as from a bottle. But is it not fitting that I, who never knew the wind of the steppe, should honor what has shaped me?"

Proceeding to the west from this emblematic grassland one reaches the first of the khan's palaces, or the first that I shall describe. It is built of wood, but of wood treated as a confectioner would sugar: the beams are slotted together in energetic criss-crossings and herringbone patterns to create towers and pinnacles of robust texture, all painted in white, blue-green and crimson; the towers being capped with domes covered by beaten gold. The servants at this palace, for each has its staff with a particular livery, are dressed in white embroidered shirts, woollen shawls and trousers, high leather boots and square-sided hats of brown fur. Their language, for each body of servants has its own, is said to be a kind of Greek, but of this I cannot speak with certainty. I might add that the palace is situated at the center of a hexagonal garden, which is divided equally by six radiating paths, so that it has the form of a flower. And the flowers within the garden are of many kinds—roses, peonies, geraniums, poppies, tulips—but all of them red.

If one leaves the precincts of this palace by the southward path and then continues, bearing perhaps a little to the left, one reaches the next great palace of the khan, which is a low building covered all over with tiles of ivory, and surmounted by a broad ivory dome. Around this palace is a trellislike wall, three feet high, faced with tiles in the same ivory color and enclosing not only the palace but also the pair of rectangular pools that extend in front of the building, one on each side of the main approach, each splashing and bubbling with a pair of fountains. As one walks toward the palace, between the pools, the gentle noise of the water may be joined by the songs of birds in the fruit trees—peach, apricot, nectarine, fig, persimmon—that grow against the walls of the principal building, inside which is a cool silent darkness. Then slowly, as your eyes grow accustomed to the light that creeps through the wood-slatted windows, you may begin to make out the zigzag designs of cream, terracotta and chocolate on the silk cushions, or the diamond shapes on the shutters, or the curlicues of gold lettering on the ultramarine walls. And you might hear from another room lazy strumming on a small guitar, or an idle flute. And someone might appear to bring you a plate of pink marzipan, or rosewater in a small brass cup.

And having taken your rest you might rise and leave this palace in an easterly direction, toward a great gleaming white mound perhaps a hundred feet high. The whiteness is artificial: a whiteness of objects brought here for no other reason than the fact of their being white, of objects cemented together all over the surface of the hillock, if they are not to be found also (who can say?) within it. As one nears one might distinguish in the heap a great shipwrecked piece of timber, bleached by salt and sun, or an elephant's tusk, or a capital perhaps carried from the ruin of an Alexandrian city, or a lump of coral indented with asterisks, or a quartz pebble, or the shell of a barnacle, all amassed without order, except at the southern slope, where wide blocks of white marble, each a little less wide than the one below, make a narrowing staircase up to the little temple of red-and-yellow painted wood at the summit. There a monk sits in contemplation, and is visited by the khan on certain feast days. You might be told the story that otherwise he has no visitors and neither eats nor sleeps, nor is he ever seen, except on rare occasions when he emerges from his cell to light incense in the bronze vessel that stands before his doorway, or to strike the large brass gong suspended in a red wooden frame behind the temple.

The next palace, still continuing eastwards, is built within a high square wall, of which each side is a hundred yards in length, so that the whole circuit is four hundred yards. Only the khan and his closest family and most intimate friends are permitted within this palace on pain of strangulation, but there are rumors that it contains a square of grass, a turreted hall of painted wood, a court of cream ceramic, a white mountain and a walled-off block, of which each side is seventeen feet in length, so that the whole circuit is sixty-eight feet.

To go beyond this would be to venture into the merest conjecture, but you might hear that the khan has plans for more constructions beyond his square mile. Foundations have been laid for a great castle in the west, so it is said, and there is talk that excavations will take place to establish a lake in the east, a lake across which pleasure craft will skim to little islands, and perhaps to the further shore.

XI

in which the book continues again and we come to a city

And so I had asked the dragoman to leave me in this quiet square, and he had done so, which was pleasing, not because I particularly wanted to be left, for I had expressed the wish without much thought, but because the wish itself had been accommodated, so that the world, even here, even in this city of Isfahan, had still seemed a place where wishes were answered, where one could be at peace, where one's being could spread and not be enclosed, as it was in meaner places, tight within the skin. And I sat for a while, allowing memories of mosques and bazaar stalls to surrender to the inner dark, forgetting the polished pink-orange copper pans that had looked like parts of some shellfish, forgetting the Turkey carpets that the shopman had turned back leaf by leaf, each leaf a new surprise, confusing one's impressions of the whole collection, forgetting even the walls of filigreed tiles and the silver and the gold and the maroon and the ultramarine of the Masjed-i-Shah, with its domed tower like a beehive and its Siamese-twinned minarets like goalposts for rugby to be played by giant angels, or rather not forgetting these things, because they are there now for me to remember, but letting them dissolve out of my present consciousness, which was all there was at that moment of me.

And then I got up from where I had been sitting and wandered back through narrow streets and alleys to the royal court, which the man had told me, though even this I did not at that moment remember, covered an area of twenty acres. And in this marigold light of a few minutes after sunset, the trees in the court looked black and ominous, and it seemed that this enormous area, surrounded by arcades repeating the same beehive pattern, was waiting for something else to inhabit it, something beyond the drily rustling leaves and the stray dogs and the nightjars and the few people who stood or walked or conversed in clusters from which a finger or a glance would shoot out in some emphatic gesture. There was an air of expectation, and I do not think I would have been much surprised if all this had been whisked away and the court filled with some other scene, perhaps a sea battle with galleons keeling in brisk water. But then my attention was taken by other water, by the high thin splashing from a faucet into a shell-shaped stone basin, and I walked the few yards to my right to where an old woman was filling brown earthenware jugs and pausing to place them in rows on a tin tray beside her.

Her dress was of the same ultramarine that had seemed so arrogant a color inside the mosque, and her face, like the texted tiles of the exterior frieze, was of a light brown inscribed with chocolate lines, but these in fans and striations, not in curls that slobbered around the horizontal and spat out diacritics. And her headcloth was of ivory linen, and covered all of her hair, except, as I could see as I approached her, for a sprig of sheer black that curved out to her left ear, where, as it became possible for me to see as I sat myself down on the other side of the faucet and basin, a flea or a tick or a louse was taking a stroll without in any way troubling her as she knelt at her task. And nor was she bothered by my arrival, nor even by my study of her from my stone bench only ten feet away from her, but kept on filling her jugs. And each time she turned away with a filled one, so the water would be liberated to splash with a higher tone into the basin, and from there to brim over silently in a plait. And each time she turned back with an empty one, so the sound would become softer and lower, echoing within the vessel and gradually rising as the water rose, while the spilling plait would diminish, then return again to its little full strength as she turned to place another slopping consignment on her tray.

And I continued to observe her until, still silent and heedless of me, she stood, and lifted the tray of jugs to place it on her head, and walked away across the court, losing not a drop, and was enveloped in the oily shadow of an alley. And I stared back into the basin, which would continue its high-toned splash and its plaited overflow until its next visitor, and which I could now see, through the furrowed water, was coated inside with a dull green deposit of mineral and algae. And it seemed to me that this was the way of the soul, to receive a constant trickle of impressions and to let go, quietly to let go, all but a little that would fasten on the sides, and stick, and stay, and become a part of the container. And I thought that contentment might come from a sufficient acquaintance with this, and not from a wish to hold more, register more. And I knew that this knowledge had come not from the water but from the woman, had been the woman's, but that her wisdom had been conveyed in silence, as is right. And then I went back to the hotel.

XII

in which he intervenes again

He slapped the now quite heartening sheaf of papers on the table.

"What the hell are you up to?" It didn't sound like the beginning of a rational dialogue. I waited, and tried to show nothing in my face.

"I was never in Isfahan. I never saw Isfahan. Our route took us rather through Yazd. I told you that: I made a particular point of the silk they weave there. And the date palms. And the game. It seemed important if this" (a scornful pause) "book is to be any use to anybody." (But it was already of use to us.) "It was only yesterday! Can't you get a few simple facts straight?" And this again didn't seem like a question expecting an answer. I remained as before, silent as the woman of Isfahan, until he reached calmer water.

"I'm sorry. I cannot fight you with words as effectively as you fight me with silence. The work, we have established, is to be a collaboration. I just cannot see why my voice in it should be so small."

"Do you suppose that mine is greater?"

"Of course."

"No. Books make their own decisions about what they include. Their minds can no more easily be read than yours, or than that of a servant gathering water in Isfahan."

"But you're even anachronistic! The Masjed-i-Shah hadn't been built when I was there—I mean when I was not there."

"Precisely." I lit another cigarette. Then more quietly he said: "I thought we might aim for truth."

"Not that again," I said, perhaps with a weariness I couldn't disguise. "Need I quote a certain governor of Judaea? As I have tried to explain, only a fool would expect the truth to fall open before him on pages of ink."

"Even a fool might reasonably expect not to be deliberately misled." He was becoming quicker at these parries. I would have to take care.

"You mistake me," I said. "There is nothing deliberate in the misleading: the book misleads me as much as it does you, or will do its readers. We are all passive victims of its deceit."

"Is there nothing we can do, no effort we can make?"

"Nothing. None. Not by this stage. We are entrammeled in a process over which we have relatively little control. We are, if you like, discovering a book which already exists, as a road exists before we travel it—though we do not know how it will continue."

"I thought we were the book's authors."

"So we are: discoverers are always authors, inventors." (I think I can speak for you in that.) But I agreed to have another go.

XIII

in which the book continues again
and a different city is attempted

And so I had asked the dragoman to leave me in this quiet square, and he had done so, which was pleasing, because I particularly wanted to be left, because, without being sure quite why, I felt the wish to be alone in this city of Yazd, with its special silk and its date palms and its abundant game. And I sat for a while, trying to remember what the dragoman had pointed out to me of the city's architecture and commerce, but few memories could be stirred, only those of the silver gleam on that famous silk, and of the man's descriptions of groves of dates, of partridge and quail on the route to Kerman. These were, no doubt, important matters, but they were not what I was searching for, and my restlessness was unabated.

And then I got up from where I had been sitting and wandered back through narrow streets and alleys to the principal square, a mean space no more than a hundred feet across, nothing to be compared with what I had heard of the royal court at Isfahan, with in the center a much-knuckled fig tree, which in this marigold light of a few minutes after sunset took on a soft deep gray, and muttered to itself in the dry rustling of its leaves, and provided a sort of housing for nightjars, for stray dogs, and even for the few people who stood in a group beneath it and smiled secretly to one another. There was an air of stillness, as if all this could continue forever, the sun not gliding lower, the light not dimming, the birds and the dogs remaining as they were, and the people also, but then my attention was taken by the high thin splashing of water from a faucet into a shell-shaped stone basin, and I walked the few yards to my right to where a young woman was filling green earthenware jugs and pausing to place them in rows on a copper tray beside her.

Her dress was of a rich ultramarine such as I had not seen in my life before, and it shone as if illuminated from within, while her face was of a light brown, smooth and itself almost translucent, like the celebrated calcite of the region that artisans fashion into vases and bowls. And her headcloth was of ivory linen, and covered all of her hair, except, as I could see as I approached her, for a sprig of sheer black that curved out to her left ear, where hung, as it became possible for me to see as I sat myself down on the other side of the faucet and basin, a jewel of gold and amethyst that swung nobly as she kneeled at her task. And as I arrived she looked up from the basin and smiled at me, just briefly and almost ironically, or complicitly, her lips unparted, and kept on filling her jug, and kept on filling her jugs without taking any more notice of me, though that did not stop my mind repeating the vision of that smile across all else, until, still silent and heedless of me, she stood, and lifted the tray of jugs to place it on her head, and walked away across the square, losing not a drop, and was just about to be enveloped in the oily shadow of an alley when she turned, and looked straight back to where she knew I must have stayed watching her, and repeated that smile before turning back and vanishing into the blackness. And I sprang to my feet.

When I reached the point where she had disappeared, I caught sight of her again, poised thirty yards along the narrow street before me, preparing to enter a house on the left, one foot on a stone doorstep, one hand at a lock, her head turned to look for my arrival, at which she stepped quickly inside. I brushed with equal speed past the shoulders of tradesmen to go after her, entered through the same doorway, unlocked, and found myself in a round-roofed passage at the end of which I could see a crescent moon shining into a small courtyard, toward which I hesitantly moved forward.

She was indeed lying there on cushions of cotton and velvet, to mention textures I would discover only later, lying with her head just to the right of my entrance and her feet almost touching the central fountain, from which water seeped soundlessly over a stem encrusted with mineral and algae. Her right hand stayed as I arrived, at the point of placing some sweetmeat between her lips—perhaps one of the renowned local pressed dates. Again, for the third time, there was that smile, now unmistakeably inviting. I advanced, and was bold enough, or foolish enough, or ignorant enough, to lie myself down on the cushions beside her, where a place seemed to have been prepared. And instead of inserting the sweetmeat, which was indeed a candied date, into her own mouth, she put it in mine, and as I chewed I laughed, and so did she, so that for the first time I saw the perfect white regularity of her teeth, and a little of her tongue, liquidly reflecting the moonlight. And then she raised herself into a sitting position, and leaned over me as she had leaned over the basin in that other court, unfastening my shirt, smiling as each button flicked out of its hole, then loosening the belt at my waist and slowly, slowly eased the trousers from my legs. And then I raised my shoulders for her to slip the shirt from my arms, my feet for her to unloose my shoes and complete the removal of my trousers, my hips for to take off my last remaining garment, which she did with flat palms moving slowly down my thighs. I was, in all ways, prepared. Another of her smiles.

And so she began her own derobement, starting with her headcloth, which now I saw was not of linen but of the excellent silk of hereabouts, and which she unpinned and then dangled over my stomach, letting a corner of the material whisper at my flesh, before repeating the movement at my shoulders, at my thighs, and then between them, where the focus of my being was coming to lie, or rather to urge, draining from my head to drive there. Then she took the silk firmly between her two hands and placed its tight edge right across my feet as if to bind them, but did not bind them, instead pulled the stretched plaything up over my legs, and over my stiff self, flattening me against my stomach to the sound of the gentle scrape of taut silk on curled hair.

And suddenly she left off from this to slip quickly from her gown, and I was aware only of two moons of flesh catching light from their scimitar sister, of a parted mouth descending to close on mine, and of a warm, smooth, wet fruit closing at the same time on where I felt myself to be. And this fruit fitted perfectly to the contours of what I was, clothed me in a welcome darkness, embraced me with a welcome nearness and completeness and responsive fluidity. And having found me, it removed itself a little, but only a little, and seemed to carry me, suck me, with it, until it moved back in a reciprocal and rippling return, and then removed itself again and returned, removed and returned, removed and returned. And I do not know which was the more overwhelming, the remove or the return, the withdrawing or the granting, the suck or the reflux, for each demanded the other, was a part of the other, in a rhythm that was quickening its pace, until the holding stayed and stayed, the fruit clasped me as I flooded into it, under the sky of Yazd.

XIV

in which he tells me
of the first of five visits
to places of interest in Peking

There was a day, a day one cherry-blossom springtime, when the
Failed Sage took me to the great library of the city, set a little
beyond the wall and approached by means of a track through
woodland: our feet crushed the previous season's beech husks
as we walked and conversed. I remarked that it seemed to me
extraordinary to place a library outside a city rather than at its
heart. His answer was that heart and head are distinguishable,
and should be distinguished. And when I asked why the library
should require such an expedition, he replied that knowledge
always proceeds from a journey. And then we were upon it, or
so I guessed, for we had turned a corner in the path and had
before us the prospect of a great circular building, perhaps two
hundred yards in diameter and of three stories in height, con-

structed of wood painted vigorously in red, yellow and green. I asked him if this was indeed the library, the goal of our journey. It was, he agreed, the exterior: but we must enter.

We did so through the nearest of the eight doorways (as I later gathered their number to be) placed at regular intervals around the library, and having entered found our passage ahead blocked by a smooth plastered wall, which we had to follow either to the right or to the left, into corridors of darkness. At this point my companion lit a taper with the aid of his tinderbox; there was no sound other than that of his scratching. We walked to the left, clockwise as it were, and occasionally paused, and soundlessly opened doors on the right in order to look in, if only for a moment, on the rooms in this ring, each with a window at the further end, a desk before the window, a scholar before the desk, and a scroll before the scholar. There would perhaps be space for a small table or two, and possibly also some shelves bearing other scrolls, or even the occasional book. I do not know how many of these rooms we looked into, nor how many we passed without slipping their latches, nor how much of the circle of this circular building we traversed, nor how many glimpses through windows I had of the black, cubic, stone construction that stood in the middle of the garden in the middle of the library, nor how many shelved halls of books, scrolls and papers we passed through in silence, these halls open right to the roof and laced with wooden staircases and catwalks along which scholars might be seen fetching and returning the objects of their studies, coming and going from their cells.

Feeling myself brought to a showplace, and yet not quite sure what it was that was being shown, and therefore uncertain how to voice the proper pleasure, I remarked, when we were in the comparatively neutral space of a corridor dully lit by the flapping little yellow sail of light in my companion's right hand, on the silence and the atmosphere of dedication. But he merely expressed surprise that I should find this worthy of comment. So I then asked if this was a specialist library or one for all the disciplines, but again I had the feeling that I was missing the point.

"It is surely both at once," he said, as if my question had for the first time led him to doubt a little what had been a self-evident truth. "Whatever the specialization, there is one goal of knowledge. However general the education, there is one route to wisdom."

"You mean," I ventured, for by this time I was no longer an ingénu in these matters, "that all learning proceeds to and from knowledge of the self."

He smiled. "That is the precise opposite of the task here being undertaken." We walked on around that slow curve, so slow as barely to be perceptible, for a further while in silence, until I commented, as tactfully as I could, and only because I felt the continuing expectation from me of some sign of understanding, on the considerable age of most of the scholars.

"Only those who possess much in years can hope to find a place here," he said.

"Do you mean," I asked, "that the texts are difficult, that this is an advanced institution?"

"Advanced it is," he said, "but there is no difficulty in what is read here, only in the reading. How could it be otherwise when here is represented every work of knowledge or imagination known to us, every history, poem, astronomy, play, travelogue, diary and calendar?"

"Then is the library reserved for scholars of a certain age?" I said, sure that somewhere here was the lead he was waiting for me to follow.

"Only by custom," he said. Then his eyes quickly turned to me and back as we walked side by side. "Come," he said, and led me out through the next point of entrance on our left, which gave into a little garden of azaleas violent in their salmon pinks and crimsons against the scarlet of the wall so near above us. At the end of the garden, placed so that we could sit there and look back at the library, was a stone bench. There we sat.

"You must know," he began, "that this is a library of unlearning. There is a current in our thought, known as Ta Yu, which holds essentially that all would be well with the world if human knowledge of it were to be obliterated. The most extreme and zealous adherents of this doctrine interpret it as an injunction to destroy everything in our cultural heritage—books, paintings, operas, even buildings such as this—and some years ago their opinions were strongly favored in official circles, or at least their destructive urges were given free rein by those to whom superior knowledge has brought only an acuter guilt. Now that wave has passed, and we return to less troubled water, to earlier and quieter matters of dispute—for you must know that the followers of Ta Yu who hold to the traditional ways are by no means agreed on what is the proper path toward the achievement of the desired object. There are, indeed, three main schools of thought, and among those here are students of all three.

"One maintains that the best means of removing knowledge is through the expression of it, and they spend their last years in writing down everything that they know. Some who are of this persuasion write only on strips of rice paper which they then eat, so that the body may complete the annihilation of what the mind has voided. Others prefer to burn their writings, and so the choice of material is not so important. Still others write with great care and skill onto scrolls of the finest paper, which they then seal with wax and lead, holding that knowledge is most effectively eliminated by imprisonment."

I remembered the white-coated scholars writing on narrow slivers, remembered seeing some slipping these into their mouths and intently chewing while their brushes raced over the next. I remembered the pink-coated scholars with their little stoves, and the red-coated scholars stretching silk-sleeved arms over tables laid with the thick cream of unfurled scrolls.

"Are these then the three schools of which you spoke?"

"No, my friend." His voice was distant and grave. "They represent three different interpretations of the same principle. Those of an alternative school maintain that the correct procedure for attaining Ta Yu consists in our unreading whatever we have previously read. Some who are of this persuasion search out every volume, every document, every poem that has passed before their eyes, and use their time here to read these things backward. Others take the view that this reversed reading produces in fact an addition to knowledge rather than its negation, since new meanings may reveal themselves. They therefore re-read in the usual direction, but reverse the process of reading, so that knowledge passes from their minds out through their eyes and into the receptive vacancy of each character they inspect."

I remembered the green-coated scholars flipping rapidly through their books backward, or quickly scanning pieces of paper that they held upside down. And I remembered the blue-coated scholars sitting and staring at books propped before them on wooden stands: never once did I see a blue sleeve reach to turn a page.

"Are these then the two other schools of which you spoke?"

"No, my friend." His voice was thinning from me. "They represent two different interpretations of the same principle. Those of an alternative school maintain that the correct procedure for attaining Ta Yu consists in reproducing within one's mind the state of the world at the time of one's birth, so that whatever one has added to the world will be consciously annulled, and the world will be able to continue as if one had never been. They therefore spend their time here in the study of our

XV

in which I wonder at his silences

Sometimes we sit for hours, across this table at which I now write while he sleeps, and say not a word. And yet he sees this as a work of dictation, chides me for the most modest embellishments, the merest literary necessities, when I've spent perhaps three days grinding a few memories out of him, like someone turning a millstone after the grain supply has been shut off. How can he expect me not to add something of my own: a little yeast, a touch of salt, a draught of water?

Of course I understand his need for privacy: there are matters on which it's only appropriate to keep silence. For instance, nothing he's said so far would counter the conclusion he spent a decade in journeying without ever once relieving himself of turds or water. I might sometimes wonder about the sanitary

histories and chronologies, imbuing themselves thoroug
the wisdom of some precise day sixty or seventy or eight
ago, achieving a mental simulation of the world as it w

I remembered the purple-coated scholars bent over s
and raising their eyes to look out through their window

"And what happens," I said, "when the contents of th
have been emptied, whether by writing, or by forgetting,
this reconstruction of the pre-mind?"

"The rule has it that each scholar is permitted to retair
his learning one element, which is the knowledge of th
that leads from the library to the place which I saw you
within the central garden."

"And what happens there?"

"Do you imagine," he said as he stood and looked do
me, "that anyone has ever ventured on that path?"

arrangements of the famously civilized Chinese, or the conveniences at caravanserais, or I might find myself speculating about how much that passed through that body, that body there under a gray blanket, is left distributed all the way from Acre to Peking, like a dotted line on a map. But of course these aren't topics I'd want to raise in a book, and in the same way I'm content to draw a veil over his erotic adventures. Writing of that kind is but a poor substitute for the real thing, even in a prison.

No, it's his other silences that disturb me, quite apart from the fact that they hamper the work. What he discloses seems, as time goes by, more and more peripheral: it's the merchant's balance sheet, made up in due order after each town. Of course, there're things I can use; but as we spend more time together, so I become more aware of what I can't know, and what he perhaps can't reveal. He vanishes into his own silences, and the book gropes for him, like a slow blind beast after prey.

Excuse me. I mean I must excuse myself. I seem to be falling into these reveries too often. No doubt it comes from listening so much to his silences. But clearly it's time for another fresh attempt, from him another consultation of his sticks. As he might say: Repose profits those engaged in building up the country and sending forth armies.

XVI

in which the book begins yet again

It was one of those perfectly windless dawns that only eastern Persia knows how to produce: the Dasht-i-Lut was doing its best for me, fulfilling all the anticipations I had gained from what others described, approximating as near exactly as I could imagine to its Platonic form. The smoke from our fire of the previous evening ascended in a thin white vertical, like water trickling upside down into a great pool of purplish blue, which faded over in the eastern quarter into a mélange of lemon and black-currant sorbets. No one else seemed to be up yet. I threw off the Kurdish rug that had covered me for the night, rose, and stretched my arms upward with the smoke, feeling wholly and entirely glad to be where I was, finally, even though the last fortnight had taken us from the fragrant sea-girt gardens of Hormuz into the most decisively inhospitable desert we would meet this side of the Chinese border. I completed my toilet, which for lack of water was more than usually rudimentary, and strode over to check on the animals while the others severally rose and packed. My mount, which I had in a sweep of unpardonable flamboyance named Bucephalus, stood ready for whatever feats of world conquering lay ahead.

To take breakfast we sat around the fire, which one of the boys had newly stoked up so that the trickle was now a foaming gray flood. Even so, each of us had his rug pulled over his shoulders, for it was yet briskly chilly. And from hand to hand we passed the goodies we had picked up from the eager-eyed grocers of Kerman: tangerines, dried dates, almonds, and a pale amber brew of tea. If only Aunt Jem had been there, picking arguments with her crochet work, it would have seemed like the aftermath of Christmas lunch.

Later that morning, as we drew breath on the further ridge, I jumped down from Bucephalus to survey the next plain to the northeast. The wind had now picked up from the west, and, having no doubt blown sand over our ashes and footprints of the night before, was tugging at the brown silk kerchief I had traded for a propelling pencil in Yazd. The cloth muttered excitedly in my ear, as if it shared my own readiness for the journey to continue, or rather to begin, for I felt now, as we were leaving the peacock domes, the dancing fountains and the shy smile of Persia, so we were at last making a real start. In Isfahan, in Yazd, even in Kerman, Europe was everywhere to be found lurking: in an overheard conversation, in a notice nailed to a market stall, in an item of machinery. The traveler, particularly if he were English, would easily be classed as another of those coming with one eye on the mosques and another on his prose. To accommodate him, there appeared to be as much a market in stories as in honey cakes, and boy porters would expect not only a tip but a reach for the camera. From this point, however, one's presence and purposes would not bring on the same tired, greedy expectations. That might cause us some delay and annoyance, but the difficulties would be nothing beside the freedom of going beyond even the memory of Europe. I leapt back into the saddle.

At the foot of the hills there was an inn: one looked down almost perpendicularly on a pair of roofs tiled in the same beige color as the sand, as if they were rectangular devices in some abstract monochrome etching, with only a patch of darker color, where in winter there might be water, and a few green sea urchins, the crowns of palms. We zigzagged down the slope to this unlikely haven, and at our arrival were greeted by the innkeeper and his wife, he in a wide white turban that implied a coiffure as luxuriant as his crinkled beard, she in a brown robe decorated rather sportingly with French lace. Europe still fingered its reach, if only through the fruits of commerce, of which there were more. Her hair was a veritable *bureau de change,* for threaded into it were coins of the most varied provenance: then or later I noticed Russian gold, products of several Persian mintings, and small change from Turkey as well as the inevitable Nicaraguan silver dollars. Since the last stop we had come only a few miles, but the carts had still to complete the descent from the ridge—they were dotted back up the hillside like sluggish memories of whence we had come—and so we decided to spend the night here. I reached into my pocket for an English shilling, which had been warming there since Dover, and presented it to our hostess to add to her collection.

Afterward I inspected the site. At the middle of the erstwhile pool, where I sauntered out over the welcome novelty of firm sand, there lay a crudely carved toy boat, the hull painted in flaking white and red, waiting both for the rains and some child. None was about, and our tinkling hostess would have been a

Sarah if she had had babes still on her hands. Possibly the thing was there, like games of Monopoly in Eastbourne hotels, to cater for the needs of passing progeny. I turned it over gently with my foot, and three fat black beetles rushed about a little before regaining their shade. So it had at least that function.

Supper was Lucullan, by desert standards. Perhaps the value of my shilling had been rather overestimated, or perhaps something in our appearance had given hope of more, but we feasted on roasted duck, some dishes of spiced vegetables and a great bowl of brown rice exhaling veils of steam. I ate greedily. Afterward enormous oranges were passed from hand to hand, circling like planets; but I do not think any of us had stomach for more. We retired to our rugs under the sky, and in the stillness of my watching Orion rose smoothly, like a man in an elevator. He at least would be a familiar companion on the way stations to Afghanistan.

XVII

in which he says nothing
of Afghanistan

Another silence. His route, as far as I could make out, skirted
Afghanistan on the northern side, taking him through some of
the more slippery pieces of the Soviet jigsaw, the republics
of the Turkmenians, Uzbecks, and Tadzhiks, all worshipers of
Mohammed, and so into China, tucking through the western
folds of the Himalaya. Disputed states—Kashmir, Tibet, Sik-
kim—fell away to the southwest like dead letters, like leaves.
There was a dream: was it mine or his? A boy, cherished as a
future warrior, squints up into the sun, wearing on his head a
stoutly embroidered silk cap (the memory is monochrome: let's
say the cap was a rich shade of ultramarine). With his left hand,
as he looks toward the traveler, he beckons and at the same
time points. Go south, he seems to say; see and report. But a

man, in a high hat as shaggy as his mustache, a rough coat tightly belted and cloth-padded feet, stands behind him. His message is to be read in the vertical grooves that spring up in severe attention at the center of his forehead. Proceed. Leave us.

XVIII

in which he tells me
of the second of five visits
to places of interest in Peking

We went on through the crisp deposit of leaves that spring,
accompanied only by the sounds of our pacing almost in unison,
severing structures in each instant that had taken months in the
building. "Where are we going?" I asked. "Toward our deaths,"
was his reply, which he made without portentousness and without humor, as if the notion were still something fresh and doubtful just emerging into consciousness. We walked on in silence,
of which our supply was always plentiful, until we seemed to
reach our destination, for we turned a corner in the path and had
before us the prospect of a bamboo stockade, with walls about
three feet high enclosing a square compound of perhaps two
hundred feet on each side. Inside there was a great crowd in
shifts and gowns and coats of lustrous silk: kingfisher blue,

plum, primrose, vermilion, nickel green. Many wore silken hats too, with black ribbons rippling from them. And the flapping of wind through silk, for at each corner of the compound was a wide breeze-curled banner bearing a picture of a mythical beast, was almost the only sound to be heard, since there was no excited chatter coming from what I could now call—for see, the bamboo construction at the right end of the stockade is a stage—an audience. They clustered and reclustered noiselessly at this point, or sat. The masks perhaps would have inhibited conversation for the moment. Ours, white-stringed in rigid white paper, were passed to us by waiting women as we reached the entrance, and I asked the Failed Sage why it should be that the audience was masked.

"Is it so strange?" he said.

"Yes," I replied. "In my country the actors might be masked, but never the audience."

"Why so?"

"Well, of course, because the actors have to present roles," I said.

"So it is in our theater."

"Whereas," I went forward more confidently, as if turning a corner in what I was able to convince myself was an argument, "the audience . . ." But then I stopped, for the hoped-for goal had curiously not come into view.

"May they interrupt?" he said. "May they cry out, fight, commit acts of indecency?"

"Well, no," I said, "but they have no parts to play."

"It would seem to me, even so, that their behavior is much circumscribed."

"Up to a point, but they are not playing characters; they are there as themselves."

"I wonder quite what that might mean," he said, and was silent for a moment. "For surely the role of spectator is quite as limiting as that of actor, and is it not right that this should be acknowledged? We put on masks as we enter the theater," and here he did so, then turned toward me with three-quarters of his face, from hairline down to just above the lips, covered by a square of varnished white, blank but for eyeholes and a shaping over the nose, "because we take on our roles as audience, and accept those roles." He put a hand on my elbow to encourage me forward into the compound. I dangled my mask from my fingers.

"But surely," I said, "the theater is not a meeting of like with like such as you describe. It is on the contrary, and most essentially, a place where the imaginary is confronted by the real: imaginary action by real spectators."

"Would it were so," he said, "but which of us can enter the theater and bring the real world with him?" We entered the theater, found ourselves adjacent chairs, and sat, while I at least looked closely at the stage. It was a square platform raised on bamboo poles, and covered for the most part with a tent or awning in cream cotton, open at the front and sides. At the back was a screen, perhaps of thick paper, with two doorways cut into it. These, my companion explained, were the Gates of the Ghosts, so called because all the characters who came through them would indeed be ghosts, people who had lived and died. All the repertory was of history plays.

And ours begins, with a hard attack struck on a wooden block and a long flute note curving upward as it dies, drawing through the left gate at a smooth shuffle the first of our ghosts. I need no help in identifying him as the villain: the eyes of his full mask are huge and bulbous, the irises completely exposed as black discs on inflated blanched almonds set in a disc of seething scarlet that otherwise is broken only by a scowling mouth, huge nostrils and a black mustache. His robe is also of red, and he wears the black cap of an official. He begins with a soliloquy intoned on a whistling, wheedling croak, a sound that might be laughable were it not so disturbingly out of proportion with the savagery out of which it issues.

"You must explain to me what is happening," I said.

"A play."

"Yes, but what does the play show?"

"Ah, I see. We are to understand that this general has long been in enmity with the house of Chao. By stratagem he has killed Chao Tun, who was his only equal in favor with the emperor; he has now planned another trick to catch the death of Chao Tun's only son, Chao Shuo. This we shall soon see succeed, as we have so soon heard the first did. Then we shall watch the general embark on a third scheme, which will take much longer to unfold: twenty years, or, in the time that we are here, five acts. The general will be led by a counterfeint to believe that he has rid the world of Chao Shuo's infant son, but the child will survive—" He stopped to admire the scene in which Chao Shuo, all in white, with black-edged eyes, like a Pierrot, stabs himself in obedience to a forged imperial edict delivered on the general's orders. The moment is quite simple and slow, a single thing that the actor extends and develops with fine care and the most minimal alteration, as water extends a touch in a circle of ripples. He sings a couple of lines in a full mellifluous tenor, then takes the knife in his right hand, kneels toward the Gates of the Ghosts, jolts his body and falls. His wife, so suddenly his widow, with an elaborate jeweled headdress and a stiff yellow robe (she is the emperor's daughter) holds up her right arm, making a clear oblique of distress that is continued by the back of her costume as it falls from below her shoulders. With a few stifled syllables she is gone. The fateful messenger, eyes cast down under his gray dish of a hat, delivers his last message to us, with effects less terrible, and exits through the other gate.

"As I say, the child will survive. Born posthumously, he is smuggled out of the house by an old family servant after the princess his mother has hanged herself. Of course, the general has the house under guard, waiting for the birth: he cannot have the emperor's daughter put to death, but he must eliminate the last heir of the Chao family as soon as the child has an independent existence, even though that child will also be a scion of the imperial clan. However, the guard owes a debt of honor to the servant, for reasons which need not concern us. The servant reminds him of his responsibility and is allowed to escape with the child. Then of course the guard, since he had disobeyed the general's orders, must kill himself. Look."

So it happens. The servant, carrying the hope of the Chao in a basket, converses with the guard: gray with red, charity with order. Then order gives way to charity when charity proves to have order in its support; but order must be true to itself, and slits its throat. The deaths, it becomes evident, are frequent but decorous, performed with solemnity and at a silent slump.

"Now," my companion continued, "the general is aware, because of the guard's suicide, that the orphan of Chao must have been spirited away,"—scarlet returns, and rages in this awareness—"and so he determines that every newborn child shall die. It is an old story, you understand. However, the faithful servant employs another piece of trickery, which becomes more than trickery when so much is invested and so much is to be won. He substitutes his own son for the heir of Chao.

"The old gentleman you see now is another court official, blamelessly dismissed on the promptings of the general. The servant begs him to take the orphan to safety while he and his son fall victim to the slaughter. But the old gentleman says no: he will take the servant's son and die with him, while the servant, being younger, must live in his long bereavement to nurture the child of Chao. So it is, as you see. The general and his soldiers seize the infant they find at the house of the old gentleman, and presuming this to be the true heir, they kill him. You see the anguish of the real parent"—gray charity clasps its face—"and the pretended disgrace of the old gentleman, who dashes his head open against the stone steps of his house. The general believes himself now to be freed of those he considered his enemies." And my companion completed his summary in time for us to enjoy the scene where the furious scarlet figure sings and stamps his feet in triumphant dance. Then there was some scattered applause, and a shifting among the audience. We had reached the intermission.

I felt it possible at this juncture to ask my companion about the other happenings within the theater enclosure. Behind us, in the rear right-hand corner, there was a booth displaying a puppet entertainment to its own kneeling semicircle of audience within the audience, and all the while, during what we had seen so far of the play, vendors had been passing up and down with trays of bright wet coconut or battered prawns or cups of some steaming infusion. These activities seemed rather to lessen than to increase during the intermission; there was even a lull in the smiling, animated dialogues that, after the first quietness, had engaged many of those present.

"I find it odd," I said, "that the plays should be so little regarded by its audience."

"Perhaps you underestimate them, or overestimate it," he said, apparently without any intention to rebuke. "Most of us here will have seen the play many times. Or others like it. There are few plays that are performed, and even fewer subjects. Indeed, perhaps there is only one, which is the bowing of the will to destiny: you have seen it already in the suicides of the official, the princess, the guard and the gentleman. You will observe it again in the vengeance of the orphan, which again must be accomplished without any exercise of will: perhaps you would say in a mechanical fashion; perhaps I would say in a necessary way. For if the orphan were to enjoy his revenge, then as a corollary the others would have to bemoan their deaths. That would never do, for it would imply some substance of feeling that was yet to be appeased. The necessary event must be accepted as necessary, not confused with praise or blame, rejoicing or regret. And since the play itself is necessary, we honor it most by accepting it without undue emotion."

"Then why should people come?"

"They do not: masks come."

"Then why should people come to inhabit those masks? I see many who must have traveled from some distance, laborers as well as grandees."

"They come, as I say, because it is necessary: how could there be a play without an audience? There are those who are able to obey the order of the mask, stay silent and submit themselves to their function: I can hardly claim to be among them. For the rest there are other diversions, which do not interrupt or antagonize the play, any more than the rotations of the planets are disturbed by the disputes of us here on earth."

"But surely people must pay attention to the play if they are to gain anything from it?"

"What could they gain beyond what they already have? Of course, the educated will take pleasure in the declamation, gesturing and singing of the principal actors, but the intensity of that pleasure will be in proportion to their familiarity with the play, and therefore their immunity to its surprise."

"But should the play not surprise at every performance? Should it not touch and teach both the educated and the uneducated, so that they go out from the theater with their sensibilities enriched and their minds changed?"

"You are asking again," he said, "for the real to be penetrated by the imaginary, the imaginary by the real. Is that not requiring too much of a merely human composition? In the interstice between the mask and the face there is nothing, and nothing may pass through this absence. But wait."

During that word "absence" a bell had been struck, and the vibration stung through his last words without decay, as it stung too through the noise of the audience and stayed as bronze in the air to announce the return of the ghosts. People came back to their seats, and the clang at last died away, effecting for a moment a hushing of the gabble to a silken tangle of whispers. Again the woodblock and the flute, again extracting from the left gate the general, whose choleric redness seems now well earned by the events of the first half.

"An irony," said my companion. "The general has adopted the heir of Chao as his own son, and plans that the boy shall inherit his titles and distinctions. Now we see the orphan for the first time, and the servant who has brought him up thus far in safety. The servant is wretched: the boy is eighteen, and it is time to blight him with his truth. His guardian leaves him with a scroll, on which are paintings that illustrate the whole sad history of the Chao clan. The boy examines the scroll and tells us what he sees there: images of violence and deception perpetrated by a man in red. He is seized with the need to kill this villain, though he does not recognize him as the general, his adoptive father, nor does he recognize the story as that of the Chao family. Listen now to his song." But I was seized with the need to interrupt.

"Excuse me, but this is precisely an example of what I had in mind: through the observation of art the boy's eyes are opened to new understanding."

The song continues, but my companion's mask prevented me from seeing if he was trying to concentrate on it. His head was turned toward the stage, toward that other mask, most natural and limpid we had yet seen, through which, in a green tenor, syllables call to the wind in the banners and in the trees and in the palisade.

"Yes, but he is young." He spoke without looking toward me, his mask staring ahead. "Should the young be a model for the old? Besides, what he learns from the scroll is undirected. See, the servant reappears and explains the images to him."

The man in gray chants at length. There has been no attempt to make him look older, and perhaps I remarked on this to my companion, and perhaps he answered that it had not been eighteen years but only half an hour since the last act. I might also have wondered about the delay to the plot caused by such a long recapitulation, for some of the story is coming round for the fourth time: we have heard it as a threat from the general, seen it enacted on the stage, understood it from the boy's description of the scroll, and are now hearing it again in the servant's explanation. But he might have answered that promise, event, allusion and report are not the same thing, and that their presence together in the play acknowledges that the world contains what is to come, what is, what remains unknown, and what was. Other things I remember more clearly.

"If I may interrupt again," I said—the gray sleeves go on swinging always at their own slow waft, whatever the speed and size of the actor's gestures, and they are often abrupt, to signify events in the long-waiting, long-unraveling revelation—"perhaps here is a better example for my case. The images are explained to the boy and so he gains wisdom. A representation is changing his life once its terms have been set out to him."

"Then is his life changed by the representation or by the explaining? Do you see the play, or do you rather see my interpretation of it?"

"But the interpretation would not exist without the play. And if you were not here, then I would be interpreting it to myself."

"And yet," there was no smile in his words, no gentle admonishment but a weariness, "I had thought you spoke of meeting the play directly, the real you to be impinged upon by the imaginary action. Who then is this other who does the explaining?"

The orpan at last recognizes himself in what he has been told and faints, then rises to sing of his newly informed and strengthened desire for vengeance: more tenor for the winds. Exit.

"The last act is comparatively short." It begins with a corpulent ghost, his stomach slopping in unwise pink silk over an unwise belt, striding forward in time with the beat of a drum. "This is another official, who will pronounce sentence. He has asked the orphan to apprehend the general in private, for fear that a public arrest would incite the army to revolt. And it is done so." For the first time bulging red and frank green meet each other on stage, and sing in their respective colors, but briefly, before the general is bound. "The sentence is that he be pinned to the wooden donkey and flayed alive, and only when every particle of skin and muscle has been eased with the blade from his body is his screaming head to be sliced off and his chest opened so that his entrails may spill. Thus order is restored."

There was no applause, and no immediate pressure to leave. The vendors were still about, and the puppet show seemed no nearer a denouement, and the gaming still clacked from squatting groups with ivory tablets around the auditorium, the gamblers also masked. But we got up, passed through the crowd to where we had come in, and abandoned our masks into gathering fingers. We returned along the path, and seemed to be the only ones taking that route, silent but for the soft crunchings of leaves that kept pace with us, until I ventured a remark.

"Should we feel sorry for the general?" He stopped, and I turned my head to look back at him as I placed a foot forward; then he smiled and continued.

"No. He will be enjoying a sound supper with the rest of the cast."

"I mean the character," I said. "His deeds were evil, his sense of correctness severely limited, but even so, to suffer such a death . . ."

"Deaths are not suffered in the theater: did you not see that things occur quite tidily, and that the actors return for their applause?" Runners clenching pale blue billowing silks, pulling curtains from right and left but looking blindly toward the audience, mirroring one another like bookends, dressed in identical dun shorts and jerkins with their hair slicked back into pigtails, chosen for a pair, possibly even twins, bring a close to each scene, and sidling through come the masked actors.

"No, I am not talking about the actors here but about the characters they portray. We are surely to imagine the general being led off to his protracted pains—"

"Not necessarily. One might say that the sentence itself is the proper ending to the play, giving the promise but not the effecting of justice. One might say that such a promise is the inevitable ending for a play, closing a movement without initiating another, for were the general to be executed in a further scene, or were his execution to be reported, as might be more likely in order to preserve the admirableness of the theater, then his family would be bound to seek vengeance in the same way that it was sought by the orphan of Chao, and a whole new play would have to start. Deaths may occur within a play, of course, as we have seen. Indeed, it is difficult to conceive of a play without unjust deaths to stimulate the operation of duty. But at the end a totally just death is required, and therefore an uncompleted death, a death that remains a promise and therefore exacts no retribution. Only in such incompletion can a play satisfactorily terminate."

"I might argue that this is true," I said, "only of plays in which all the characters are dead from the beginning, as are your ghosts." I pitched my words to a tone of hypothesis that I hoped would not offend my companion, for at that time I still had little comprehension of how far he was from any extension of pride into our discourses. "And in a sense you have answered my question about the excessiveness of the final judgment, since it would be wrong to feel sympathy for characters who exist only in a pattern and do not express feeling."

"But were you not listening to the songs? The princess's lament, the general's rage, the orphan's recognition of his duty: these were things exactly delineated."

"That I can countenance as you describe it," I said, "though I fear my knowledge of your musical and dramatic arts is too restricted for me to have any fine discrimination of the affections they present."

"Indeed," he said wonderingly, and then: "It occurs to me that perhaps the sorrow, anger and zeal I mentioned may be particular to our theater, if their expression seems to you so foreign."

"Does one consider," I asked, "that the inhabitants of India must have different hearts because one does not understand their language?"

"Most certainly not, but if I learn their language then it may be I who has the different heart. Because I have two different ways of expressing 'envy,' shall we say, each associated in my mind with different persons and anecdotes, then I have two quite different envies. I force a distinction in myself by learning a different means of expression; whereas one might say that the Chinese who has no other language and the Indian who has no other language both share the same concept. We must be wary of the notion that knowledge of another's culture takes us closer to him: unless we are circumspect it may drive us irrevocably further away. We must be wary therefore of making comparisons between cultures."

"You are right, as always," I said, "to alert me to some danger in my thinking. And yet I feel there is a real difference between your theater and ours, a difference so fundamental that I cannot believe it to be chimerical, created in my mind by a difference in means of expression. In your plays the progress of the action is never in doubt: the characters follow their courses like figures on an astronomical clock."

"Is that not morally irreproachable, that their behavior should be correct and free from selfishness?"

"Yes indeed, but it is an ideal and not an image of behavior. Life is an experience of doubt. Your characters do not doubt, and therefore they do not live."

"Of course not," he said, "they are mouthing words written for them, in a study by candlelight, brushed in black on a scroll of white paper by a thick-fingered right hand while the left slaps at insects: did you not see Chi Chunhsiang biting his nails in the second row at the general's grosser improvisations?" I shook my head. "But come," he continued, "am I to understand there are no scripts in your theater? Are the characters no less puppets of the playwright's manufacture?"

"Of course there are scripts," I said, "but we would judge a play by the degree to which the fact of there being a script is effaced in performance, so that the play becomes the necessary actions and thoughts of particular people, so that the characters seem to be speaking for themselves."

"Then they may choose their own words?"

"No indeed, it is rather that those words have chosen them, because the words have created them."

[In another version of this conversation there is an interpolation at this point, the speech continuing with the words: "The words create a sense of time passing as our time passes, unique for the characters as our time is unique for us, and because of this the characters are unique as we are unique. They can make choices, feel and suffer, because they exist in their time as we exist in ours, knowing no other. Time unfolds for them as inexorably as it does for us, without the leaps and stops of your theater."

"But suppose you were wrong in your suppositions about the nature of time. Suppose your scholars and philosophers were to discover that time is only an illusion of consciousness, the illusion a falling leaf might entertain that upper must always come before lower, because that is the way it falls, not seeing, because not being, the mass of things in the universe for which movement is otherwise? If you have tied your aesthetics to a theory of time, how will you fare when your theory is undermined? Would it not be better to have a drama that is known to be artificial, but known also to be efficacious, rather than one that claims a grounding in truth that may be falsehood?"

He paused, and I was silent, and he went on: "Moreover, your claim to truth may be a cause of arrogance. You would have to conclude that others err, that our theater is a travesty of yours, a fruit of ignorance and weakness of thought, or perhaps some would even say of passionlessness and a lack of humanity. Or else you are forced to the view that our theater is different because our view of the world is different, and therefore that different views are possible, and therefore that yours has no particular guarantee. But I would rather put the case differently. What you see on your stage is what you think you are. What I see on my stage is what I know I am not." And he stopped again for a moment. "We must think some other time about whether it would be advantageous to either of us to attempt to accommodate the other's point of view."

"But wait," I said. "Our theater is justified not by metaphysics but by experience. We see lives lived as ours are lived."]

"So you are willing victims of a trick. In fact your characters have no free will, as you suppose you have, but only a semblance."

"But the fact of semblance vanishes! That is what makes the

theater worthy of our attention, of our address of ourselves, without masks. We measure an author's skill by the life he can grant his characters, and an actor's by his ability to render that life. The gifted author and the gifted actor can bring the dead to life. The great author and the great actor can do so while also showing us themselves."

"It seems to me," he said, "that our theater is so much more realistic. You praise your theater as the shadow of your life: is that not a kind of egoism? I praise our theater as the reality of itself. But I am reminded, when you speak of the great actor being perceived both as himself and as his character, presumably without the two natures being separable, so that we might say that in a certain gesture he was himself while in a certain intonation he was his character—" He waited for confirmation.

"No, the fusion would certainly be a criterion of the truly great performance."

"Then I am reminded of your Christ, and I wonder if all your theater is not fundamentally, like ours, a religious revelation, so that the differences we have discussed are differences of religion. Or there may be deeper causes yet, of which religion and theater are merely manifestations."

"You mean," I said, "that Christ was a man who took on the role of God. That is not—"

"Of course not. You will forgive my interrupting, but I would never be guilty of such a blasphemy. No, Christ was, as each of us is, as every created thing is, divine. His awesome folly was to play the part of a man."

XIX

in which the book continues yet again and I approach Samarkand

Shimmering Samarkand lay shimmering on the plain ahead, doubly shimmering because the late afternoon's brilliant reflections from the domes would have jigged any attempt at a steady gaze, and because the dance of eyes and light, impossible to end, was complicated by another, quicker dance of light and haze. The light itself was clear yellow, as if the alchemy of the sun's gold and the copper of the domes had produced flaming sodium, such as I had seen spluttering in my childhood when my father had thrown salt into the drawing-room grate in a vain attempt to check the roar of a chimney fire at the house in Somerset. Except that in that case there had been, I suppose, a good reason for the color, whereas here the same yellow was, in point of its sameness illusory, and therefore in a third manner shimmering.

I was approaching the city on a gray gelding I had acquired from the beefy chatelaine of the night before, in return for some Russian silver and an hour spent hearing of her son's exploits over virulent cups of thick sweet coffee. I had wanted to ride into Samarkand like an emperor, not drive or be driven or stumble from the night express: cities impose their own means of encounter, and it would be as crass an affront to arrive in Samarkand by Land-Rover as to take the bus to Venice. But the physical necessities are always easier to handle than the mental. I had, of course, no guidebooks with me, and no maps to spin like spiders their own delineations over the contours of those palpitating roofs and towers. And Flecker I had superstitiously wrapped within a blanket four thousand miles away. But a line of Marlowe, coming forward to greet the galloping ten-act rogue's tomb, kept recurring in that growling grandeur only Wolfit could get away with:

To entertain divine Zenocrate

and I found myself, with the rhythm of the horse and equally beyond much control, inventing pentameters to go with it, since I had no memory of what the detestable Kit had really made Tamburlaine promise:

A rope of coral and a twist of pearls
A cagèd king that I will make my sport
Some hundred monkeys of an Afric tribe
Silks of Cathay and condiments of fire
Broad gilded domes that teach the sun to burn.

So much for entering Samarkand as I had planned, nude as a child. But perhaps that had never been very realistic. Perhaps the only way to see Samarkand in innocence would be to come upon it unexpectedly and not to recognize it, passing through its groves and gardens and squares and yelling lanes not knowing where one was; not startled into awareness even by its mosques that bring the blue calm of the sea a thousand miles inland, as if Mohammed would have here a mirror to the lapping Mediterranean at the other end of his imperium; not nudged to remember even by the mausoleum of the mighty Tamburlaine himself. Or perhaps one would have to visit some other city as if it were Samarkand, to go, let us say, to Birmingham, and see in Corporation Street a souk for laquerware, dried figs, inlaid coffers and copper pans bright orange-pink like parts of shellfish, or see in the Delphic town hall the monument of one who slaughtered worlds but entertained his queen.

XX

in which he intervenes yet again

I don't know how many days have written themselves into these pages he holds, as he slips another from the top to the bottom of the pile in his left hand, and skips his appraising eyes up while his mouth stays tightly downturned in disapproval, the disapproval I've learned to expect and he to express. I can't accommodate him. My only hope now is that he'll take up pen himself, and discover how impractical his requirements are. Indeed, he's already begun, when he thinks I'm asleep, begun to tease out words or sentences on scraps of paper which he then burns in the candle flame. Perhaps he'll eventually come to satisfy himself with his efforts, and cover sheets that can be added to the store. If he does, I'm certainly not the one to object on grounds of professional pride. All my own work? Hah! Let him scribble away. (Of course, at this point I still didn't realize how far from innocence he was in these matters. He hadn't yet told me his stories of the Guardians of Knowledge, the Game of God, and the Breaker of Categories.)

But I don't know how many days we've been here. We've not been making scratches on the wall, none of that, grating a line for each dawn, or for each visit of the only other human being we ever set eyes on—I call him the dainty alligator for his mincing manner, his spotless neat-folded red worsted and the sleek, jaws-unparted, lips-retracted grin that's the nearest he comes to conversation with us in this hellhole—when he comes to slosh the contents of our bucket somewhere out in the corridor, presumably through a window, and to bring more bread, water, occasionally wine, or an onion, and paper, always more paper, and a fresh pen, and ink. Another page, another quick vertical dash of the eyes to maintain the scanning horizontal that leads through . . . Samarkand: is that where he is? Impossible to read his location in those eyes.

And a mosquito is in the cell with us: one feels an immediate fellowship even with such visitors, even with the alligator. One even goes so far—does one not?—as to take their point of view, simply for the change from the usual two. So with the insect him—or it's more likely to be her, that'll be a novelty—I look down. And is she so used to her circling that her eyes or brain make some compensation for it, so that she sees two gray heads stable on either side of a table beneath her wobbling elliptical rotations? Or is there no allowance made, so that the heads and the table spin more or less eccentrically? If the former, might she imagine that there is only one head and a cunningly positioned mirror, since from above our two greasy, bedraggled, bald-spotted, thick-skinned skulls must look pretty identical? Or perhaps not, if one has developed discernment from a lifetime of looking down. But if we're being seen as moving in mad circulations, the mirror idea would seem less tenable, for a spinning mirror would suggest incipient catastrophe, which is not to be supposed. And of course, while my eyes are raised to her and his lowered, lowering to the page, we're not going to look like object and reflection at all.

But then he places the pages flat on the table between us, and stares across at me, and my eyes meet his, restoring symmetry. And because my mind has been in the mosquito's head and not in my own—because, too, through these unscored days I've been looking so much at this other face I know it better than my own—for a moment I'm unsure whether I'm Rustichello looking at Marco or Marco looking in a mirror. To mention only those possibilities. And the fizz of wingbeats stops, and I wonder if I'll soon know, if I'll feel the bite and watch the grimace I make. But there's only the pain, while the lips almost touch a smile as they open in sad-soft sounds.

"So, Samarkand. No matter that I saw as little of its markets as of Isfahan's. No matter. I begin to see I must content myself with following your journey as much as you follow mine. Let us simply hope we can agree on the same destination and find a pleasant route."

"As I've tried to explain," I said, "our journey is largely plotted for us."

"Now no more of that, my friend. You have already proved in Yazd that you can turn the course of events and take them toward your own fantasies. One thing, though, I will allow: truth is not to be on our itinerary. But perhaps there is in that a kind of realism. If we strive for truth, we are bound to lie. Whereas if we set out instead to produce a fabrication . . ." He turned toward the door. "If one has regrets, I suppose they are a sort of egoism." And in a more incisive tone, his attention returning to me: "But what about my father and uncle? They disappeared rather abruptly from the story, did they not?"

I picked up the manuscript and ruffled back through the pages. "Indeed, I had forgotten about them myself . . ." I found the place, and made a note that emendations would be necessary. They'd be necessary all the way through. "However, I think it's all for the best that their roles should be, shall we say, relatively minor."

"But no, they were the leaders of the expedition. I was only a boy on the outward trip, and even on the return journey I of course deferred to them. They knew much more of the country than I did. They'd made all the contacts."

"Of course, but history has a weak memory for names: one in most cases will do. Can we expect children at their bustling desks to remember that Niccolò and Maffeo and Marco Polo all made the journey to Peking?"

"I thought we had agreed," he said, "that we are writing a fable and not a history."

"I thought we had agreed the two are indistinguishable."

"Not quite," he said. "Most desperately not quite. We may have turned our backs on truth, but it is still there. It still exists as the ideal of those who would attempt a faithful record."

"You speak of chronicle," I said, "of the dates of battles, kings and popes, the numbers killed, begotten and canonized, the prices of swords, silence and simony, the weights of corpses, jewels and truffled peafowl, the colors of death, death and death." (More embroidery: for your benefit, of course.) "If you'd kept meticulous notebooks on your journey, then perhaps you might have offered us something of this kind." (I made the point a little acidly.) "But since you were so often the only Latin witness to events—" (I raised my hand) "for the moment I exclude your noble father and uncle—why the hell should we trust you? Even if we accept your honesty, you may have been misled. You may have forgotten what happened. You may have dreamed what you think you experienced. In any event, as soon as we make chronicle into history, put life into death, motives into deeds, then we commit falsehood. And we'd do better to make it a conspicuous falsehood, which confuses no one, rather than a falsehood we dress up" (I was moving forward with what I hoped look like fearless determination) "because we want to congratulate ourselves on our virtuousness in telling the truth." I thought that might keep him quiet for a while, but I was wrong.

"Well spoken, Rustichello. You set my mind at rest, at least for the moment. I am persuaded that lies can be scrupulous: you echo others who spoke perhaps from different motives, but to the same effect. Who can tell, though, what their motives were? Or indeed, my friend, what yours might be?" He slapped the table. "But come, is it merely an economy that my father and uncle should have to vanish from the narrative?"

"Not merely. The first person singular, you see, is also a convenience to our readers: it is a narrow window in a white wall through which they climb themselves. And though there may be a limit to their self-insertion—for instance, if they differ from the narrator in sex or appetites—I think it never very disabling, so clamorous are they to possess the pronoun that is always theirs alone."

"Very well, my friend," and he almost laughed, "let us and our readers proceed. I think we should all have another try at Samarkand, which perhaps should have been Shibarghan or Balkh."

"And perhaps after that we should try a new style," I said. "I feel I still haven't found the right voice for this 'I.' "

"You mean me?" And then he did laugh. "I laugh, do I not, at my own execution. For far from being any statement or expression of myself, this 'I' of the book is a dissolution into a mentality that will be reshaped on someone else."

(I do begin to doubt the reality of my own reporting.)

XXI

in which I attend a public execution

The gong it was, crashing five minutes before the promised event, that introduced the note of solemnity. Otherwise people were behaving very much as they would at a similar occasion in Europe: there was a great press of observers around the scaffold, perhaps a couple of hundred of them two or three deep hugging the shoulder-high platform on which stood the executioner, the physician, the accuser and the victim, and then the remainder of the square was more evenly sprinkled with family groups, bevies of young friends, solitary spectators, one or two hurrying to be gone, hurrying the more in the resonance of the gong. And of course there were the subsidiary attractions. A man in glossy royal blue with vermilion piping—it might have been a military uniform—was standing with head leaned far back and mouth open while his eyes, tightened against the light of the sky, flickered from one to another of three white plates his hands kept tossing into the air. A purveyor of some root, which looked like the hybrid of a parsnip and a gorgon, had a trestle table and his own small band of watchful auditors as he sang in deep gutturals. Three boys with bleached hair were gaining some attention for their skill at weaving through the mob on wheeled boards. But the gong, crashing from a tower that overlooked the square, had turned most eyes to the dais, and as its sound bulged then stayed, then slowly filtered away to leave a low horn tone, so the noise of anticipatory chatter, even the noise of the hawkers, reached its climax and lessened. Then again the gong to mark the beginning of the proceedings, or rather the beginning of the end of them, and to initiate some explanation from the Failed Sage beside me.

"He with the long mustache who steps forward a pace now," (he was a short man whose large stomach slopped in unwise pink silk over an unwise belt, and he made his step wobbling with portentous formality) "is the public accuser, who must read out the details of the crime. It is, I am afraid, in this instance a rather mundane affair. A woman had been going for twenty years to pay her respects at the tomb of her parents, until one day she met there an old man, loaded with flowers and candles and incense sticks and sweet yellow cakes, who said that the plot she had been venerating was in fact the site of his son's burial, which he had been unable to visit for many years, because he had been serving in an official position in the west of the empire, and there was no one else in his family left to carry out the duties of kinship. Thereupon the woman pushed the old man so that he dashed his head on the long unattended, long wrongly tended tomb; then the same night she invited the gravedigger to supper and poisoned him."

"A sorry tale," I said. "But surely the person bound hand and foot on the scaffold and clothed in a white cotton gown is a man."

"So it would appear."

"But did you not say that the murderer was a woman?"

"Yes, indeed," said my companion, "but there is no ordinance that the malefactor and the executed should be of the same sex."

I stopped for a moment. "But surely we're talking about the same *person,* are we not?"

"Only up to a point," he said. "The one to be executed has been chosen to complete an action made necessary by the one who murdered, and so in that sense they are one person, as husband and wife may be said to be."

"Chosen?"

"I speak inprecisely. The choice is made by a soothsayer, and so may be said to be no choice at all but only a random selection. There was once the idea that the soothsayer, like a marriage broker, would find the individual best suited for the case, but I do not think anyone believes that any more."

"But surely," I said again, "the one who performed the murder ought to be the one to be executed?"

"Why so?" he said, and then: "But we must continue this conversation afterward, since the beheading is about to take place."

So we did. "The murderer ought to have been the one to be executed," I said, "because she was responsible."

"At the moment when her hand's strength was felt by the old man, who gasped and lost his footing, and at the moment when that same hand placed a pinch of white powder in the gravedigger's soup, then indeed she was responsible. But is she now?"

"Yes. She is the same person, with the same hand."

"Suppose that out of remorse she had cut off that hand?"

"It would make no difference: her guilt resides not in her hand but in her head."

"And how shall we see it there? What if she were to deny any feeling of guilt? What if she were, perhaps again as a result of remorse or else because of some illness, to have lost her memory?"

"She would still be the same person," I said.

"How may we know? Simply because we are speaking to the same body? But the person, to use your word, may have become quite different. Suppose there is an interval between the crime and its detection: the murderer may meanwhile have entered a monastery, or learned a foreign language, or read a book, or written a book, all of which might bring about quite drastic changes."

"Yet that did not prevent this particular murderer from imputing guilt to the gravedigger after twenty years."

"But I did not say that her action was correct. Indeed it was not, for murders are achieved not by persons but by wishes, and those wishes are extinguished by the act of murder as surely as is the victim. Moreover, if there is any legacy of murder in the soul of the murderer, it is less likely to be one of responsibility than of chastening. The lady in this case will no doubt be able to find ways of limiting her sense of responsibility, even though she went beyond the bounds of what is admirable or even permissible in the righting of a grievance. But she may think more carefully next time."

"Why then is it necessary for someone to be executed?" I asked.

"To complete the action. Murder cannot be allowed to happen without redress: that would be anarchy. An unlawful death calls for a lawful death to answer it. Therefore a victim must be found."

"A scapegoat."

"No, that would suggest the responsibility is being shifted onto him, which would be grotesque. He is not blamed. He simply must die. So must we all."

"Except that his life is being shortened through no fault of his own, while the person responsible lives on."

"My friend, we have already decided that responsibility is a doubtful concept; so also is fairness. In the realm of being there has been a murder, and now in compensation there has been an execution, from among those who, through their participation in the world of being, were all, if you like, responsible."

The square was emptying, and we joined others taking one of the main thoroughfares out of it, as the setting sun soaked orange onto the rightward sides, edges and arcs of their black silk hats.

"Remind me," he said, "to take you to the postmortem."

XXII

in which the book continues yet again
and I reach Shibarghan

Shimmering Shibarghan lay shimmering on the plain ahead,
doubly shimmering because the midday sun was boiling the
lower air, so that through this silent excitement the city trembled
like a reflection in water, or like a flame, and also because of a
certain haziness in my mind about whether indeed this was
Shibarghan. From a distance of about two miles the place had
the appearance of an insubstantial shadow in the insubstantial
color of mushroom soup eaten at a befogged window in the North
British Hotel. I had, of course, no guidebooks with me, and no
maps to spin like spiders their own delineations over the contours of those palpitating roofs and towers. But I thought I
recognized from the old Afghan's description a certain bell-
shaped dome that was beginning to sever itself from the indis-
tinctness as I neared, starting to cut a dash of individuality by

virtue of the warm brown metallic sheen that contrasted with the prevailing dimness of shape and texture. It was as if the alchemy of the sun's gold and the tarnish of the dome had produced drumming bronze. The thing was gaining solidity.

I was approaching the city on a skewbald gelding I had acquired from the eagle-beaked innkeeper of the night before, in return for some Russian paper money and an hour spent hearing of his exploits over fragrant cups of iced mint tea. I had wanted to ride into Shibarghan like an emperor, not drive or be driven or stumble from the night express: cities impose their own means of encounter, and it would be as crass an affront to arrive in Shibarghan by lorry as to take the train to Pisa. But perhaps I should have been equally punctilious about the route, and listened more carefully to the old Afghan, followed the waverings of his arms as they flapped and reached and shuddered like those of a puppet. Of course, there was a sense in which I did not mind whether this was Shibarghan or not: it looked to be worth a detour, as more features of the mosques and fortifications began to stabilize themselves. My only problem would be in meeting up with the others if this was not Shibarghan. But that could wait.

And so I entered this city of white-tiled façades and mahogany brick and furtive glances, still not sure where I was. I found an inn just outside the curtain wall, and gave my horse to be taken in for watering. Inside, in a sort of office that smelled of cats and sour cheese, I tried to raise the question of where quite this was, but without seeming unduly foolish—tried to say something that would leave the name of the city hanging nonchalantly in the air, as if I might inadvertently have mentioned somewhere else, perhaps the place I had been the night before, or would be the following night.

"I have heard," I said, "of the great Friday Mosque of Shibarghan."

But I cannot think my studied distractedness was very convincing.

"Shibarghan?" the woman said,.and again, getting up and knocking back with a clack on the brick floor the stool on which she had been seated: "Shibarghan?" Then clutching me by the shoulder she pushed me, with more vim than one would have supposed possible, out under the arched doorway with her into the street. "Shibarghan? Shibarghan?" She released the corrugation of her nails from my jacket, and with a hooked right forefinger pointed back down the street to the right, along the line of the city wall, which stood as mindlessly primped up as a cake frill with little windows and crenellations. "Shibarghan? Shibarghan?" The finger was gesticulating with regular urgency, and I understood I was to go along the street and take the first turning on the right. I nodded, not because I knew at all what I would find there, but rather because the woman's eagerness was being so forced upon me that I could hardly say I would see the Friday Mosque some other time. There was no alternative but to go through with it. Besides, her repeated callings of the name, which sounded like a wedge of nutty turrón in her gnashing contralto, suggested it was perhaps not the city in which she ran a low boarding house. Possibly I had indeed taken the wrong route.

Then, when she was satisfied I had taken in the matter of the right turn, she stopped jabbing at the air and held up two fingers, or rather thrust them up with the same vibratory drive. "Shkaht, shkaht." The fingers juddered, and the woman's eyes bore into me. "Shkaht, shkaht."

"Shkaht," I said. But this did not seem to be quite enough. "Shkaht," I said again, and held up two fingers myself. She relaxed her hand to touch me on the elbow and went inside. There was nothing to do but go along and try to follow the directions.

The right turn, if it was indeed the correct right turn, took me into an alley that curved torward the left and was empty of people. Blocks of stone a foot high raised a narrow flagged pavement along the left side, on which there were entrances and occasional windows in the rendered wall, while on the other side was only a featureless face of pitted plaster. I presumed the number two had been signaled to me, and was just standing to wonder whether this might mean I was to venture into the second doorway when there leaned out from that entrance a man in a striped white and gray cloak and a red hat, who saw that I was there, made a quick beckoning gesture with his arm, and disappeared back inside. I followed diagonally across the street, stepped up onto the pavement, and went as he had summoned.

He was waiting for me at the top of a flight of stone steps leading down to a cellar, and I felt my way cautiously in the gloom as I tried to keep pace with the pattering of his bare feet. At the bottom was a doorway again, with a woven curtain that he held back for me. I went inside, alone, and found a chamber with a ruby carpet draped over the stone floor, and three or four oil lamps burning to reveal a rug-covered divan liberally bedecked with cushions, a honeywood chest and a wooden ceiling painted in violent chevrons of red, green and white. The first thing that surprised me about the boy as he entered was his pallor; the second was the triangular flatness of his face, whose high cheekbones (for his gray-yellow straight hair, too, he might have been a German or a Balt) seemed to stretch his small mouth permanently open; the third was the very marked unequalness of his testicles, forming in smooth carnality an iamb.

XXIII

in which the book continues yet again
and I come too late to Balkh

Shimmering Balkh lay shimmering on the plain ahead, doubly shimmering because the early morning sun was defying all my efforts to strain my eyes eastward, making my vision leap around the place where the city might be, and also because I was not at all sure there was anything there to be seen. The Arabs had called her "mother of cities," but perhaps she had been exhausted by so many births, and having finally been delivered of Brasilia and Milton Keynes lay emptied and in disarray. Genghis Khan (or was it Tamerlane? Check) had passed this way, and played thunder with the walls of forts and palaces. More recently the lapping tides of Persians and Russians had continued the ruining, so that little was to be expected: the guidebooks spoke only of desolation, and the place had slipped the ungenerous memory of maps. And though I thought I could discern a few rough shapes on the skyline, it might have been the alchemy of the sun's gold creating something out of nothing.

I was approaching the city on a black gelding I had acquired from the boy at the caravanserai of the night before, in return for some Russian hashish and an hour spent hearing of his father's exploits over insipid cups of lemonade. I had wanted to ride into Balkh like an emperor, not drive or be driven or stumble from the night express: cities impose their own means of encounter, and it would be as crass an affront to arrive in Balkh by minibus as to drop by helicopter upon Genoa. But perhaps I should have been equally fastidious about keeping my ignorance intact, for if one can be wrong-footed in one's meeting with a city by inappropriate transport, so can one be by anticipation. And my head was positively echoing with tales of Balkh past.

According to one story it was from Balkh that the magi set out, and traveled perhaps very much along the road that I had taken, though going in the opposite direction to keep faith with their star. With what hope, I imagined, they would have passed through this space I now occupied, their preparations at last completed, their gifts stowed, their journey just begun, their eyes held by the point that gave a meaning to the scattering disorder of the heavens. And really this is more than a story, because Balkh had been the citadel of Zoroaster, the originator of that terrible good news that Christ then amplified for the world, the news that man is perfectible, that the universe can be made better, that each rise of the sun, each step of a horse, each beat of a heart brings the millennium nearer. Except that Zoroaster was not heir to the Old Testament doctrine of sin, but taught that evil lay in the lie, that untruth must be rolled back like a heavy carpet by the strenuous exertions of men and women, or like the clinging peel of a fruit, until at the last day the world should stand nude as a child, and be seen for the first time in entireness of truth.

I wondered if Zoroaster would have been surprised, returning twenty-five centuries later, to find his city laid low, his teachings appropriated, and the world so very little advanced on the road to salvation. He had expected that lies would gradually be consumed by the god of light and fire, like slips of paper vanishing into flames, whereas in fact the empire of deception had continuously extended its reach. Yet perhaps he would have felt himself justified by the history of science, and surely he might gain some gentle delight from the notion that the world did indeed begin in an instant of fire. But what of that other notion that the universe is as it is only because it contains us to see it, that the primeval fire could have been formed and developed in countless ways, that infinite alternatives must be countenanced as a part of reality? Perhaps, after all, other religions were more realistic in discovering the root of evil not in the lie but in knowledge.

So Zoroaster had ruled, and his banner, planted deep in the substrata of a city already old, had been winded eastward by the gust of Alexander, marrying here his Roxana and going on to India, then westward by the returning boy, kicking the dust of this same plain in haste and rage that the world had cheated him, not offering a limit to his conquering but only opening itself ever more to the east, opposing no resistance but that of continued extent. And then the banner had ceased its fluttering, because the truth had been spirited away in three satchels by night: the incense of approach, the gold of possession, the myrrh of disappointment; the three qualities of knowledge. And then the Arabs had come, and finding in Zoroaster a shadow of their own prophet had obliterated him, for what men seek most to destroy is not the lie but the parallel truth.

But just before the arrival of the scimitars in patient easeful Balkh, when the chants of the Zoroastrians could still be heard in deep monotones that made the flames on their altars dance, when there were still some magi to garner stars from high towers and look for other signs, in those evening times, in the year 633, a traveler from China came, and said that this city contained three of the most beautiful buildings in the world. What he said they were is not recorded. Perhaps the great temple of Zoroaster himself, with its central fire reflected in perpetually fainter, smoother orange from marble wall to marble wall in its honey-comb of chambers. And perhaps the dwelling of the Bactrian king, where arcades of Corinthian columns harbored winged beasts in stone. And perhaps the steepled observatory, where priests could measure their failing eyesight against the luminosity of stars that so soon the Arabs would arrive to name. Or perhaps the Chinaman would have been most impressed by those buildings that reminded him of his distant home: a wall across the hills, there merely to restrain sheep; a house with a curved wooden roof; a turret that seemed the far overtone of a pagoda.

When I had at last arrived among the overthrown columns and the tumbled ashlar, and when I had fended off a boy who wanted to sell me two obvious fakes as Alexandrian coins (a farthing and a half crown for size, both smelling sweaty from the casting), I wondered what buildings I would place here to fulfil the Chinaman's boast: the cathedral of Chartres to settle its buttresses on a square paved by the Persians, a Granadan court discovered around a corner, and spanning the hills the Golden Gate Bridge. Or perhaps the most excellent buildings are those one has not seen and never will see, and so let Balkh contain King Solomon's temple, the castle of Ys, and the chiefest wonder of the next new city.

XXIV

in which I hear of his return

"Hi there! It's Marco . . . Marco! . . . Marco Polo? You know, Venetia High and all that? . . . You see, I just got back, and I was kind of . . . Oh, she was *just great*, I mean because . . . No . . . No, she hadn't—but anyways, how *are* you? . . . Well, I'm real good too, and it's so good to be hearing you again after . . . Well . . . Well hold on now, I mean we're talking like Paleozoic here, right? I mean that was just aeons ago, and . . . Yeah, really that is not a problem for me any more . . . Right . . . Right . . . No, I can safely say . . . I can safely say . . . Right . . . Well, you know, you go away, you get a lot of things sorted out . . . Right . . . I mean, this is not the old Marco Polo, you know? . . . Oh, Mommy? . . . Yeah, I was just going to tell you . . . Oh, she was just so *won-der-ful*. She was just so

pleased. I mean, this was big reunionsville, and she was, she was
. . . Yeah, she was . . . *Real* pleased, and she . . . Oh, she just
. . . She just . . . Oh, you are *so right.* She was . . . Yeah, like
we set it up so that I went in first, and all that, and I just said:
"Hi, Mommy!" And she just turned around, and she knew right
away . . . Yeah, even though I have like this beard now, and all
of that . . . Well, you know, I figured . . . Yeah, kind of more
masculine, you know? . . . But she knew right away. I guess
mothers have like these instincts and . . . Yeah . . . Yeah, she
was just *so pleased,* I mean she was *delighted,* it was . . . Yeah,
it was like it went beyond words, you know? . . . No, right, well
I must too . . . Sure, but we really must make a date . . . I know
. . . I know, I know . . . Sure, I know how it is when you have
kids and all of that . . . Sure . . . Well, I'll be hearing from you
then . . . Sure . . . And love to you too, and to . . . Yeah, bye!"

A crossed line, of course. I put the phone down. The moment
was come for another change: from him the shaking, choosing
and placing of sticks, and the words: "Integrity. Sublime success!" Integrity! What a hope. I picked up the newspaper the
alligator had slipped us with his grin.

XXV

in which I read of another beginning

For our Turkic driver the day had begun badly. The engine had coughed its unwillingness to get going in the thin air of the western Himalaya. Then after only a mile we had been obliged to wait for two hours while a choreographed platoon from the Pakistani army lazily cleared a fall of rocks.

Meanwhile our driver stayed in his seat, drumming his fingers on the wheel and occasionally giving a honk when he saw a soldier standing idle. Which would bring the offender and two or three others to the cab for exchanges of curses and so cause further delay.

Very possibly it was all a ploy to distract the military from thinking to search the Land-Rover, for the drivers no doubt make more out of contraband than they do from ferrying tourist parties over the high threshold into China. Or perhaps the man was just impatient.

I, however, had all the time in the world. I strolled from the vehicle to stare up at the peaks. It was as if God had made a mistake of scale. There was me, and the soldiers, and the lorry and the Land-Rover and the long wide road, and occasional plants and boulders all in proportion. But all around the mountains bulked excessively, dwarfing even the clouds, whose shadows scudded over them.

Nobody could have failed to be awed by the view, but there was something slightly ridiculous in the overload of bigness. These were nouveau-riche mountains, puffed up beyond their due size: perhaps they might at any moment go pop. I laughed cheerily into the west wind and returned to my seat.

The road to the border is a highway one might have imagined was taking one toward Birmingham rather than Kashgar. The sobering explanation, of course, is that the road was built for defence purposes. So those stone-gathering soldiers had more business here than me. Perhaps to punish the driver for his presumption, fate prescribed a third torment of the morning, and a tire went flat as we neared the frontier.

Border formalities, though, lost us no more time. The official outriders of the People's Republic smiled and nodded at our papers. Their inspection of the vehicle was halfhearted. And so we proceeded, and reached before dusk another of those inns where we could feast and sleep before journeying on.

Apart from the fact that there is now a glaring petrol pump instead of an ostler, the caravanserais on this highest corner of the ancient route have outwardly changed little since merchants brought stuffs for the costume balls of Heliogabalus, and took back who knows what in return: gold, olive oil, agates carved with cameos? It might help if I could discover what the Chinese called the Silk Road, but nobody I ask can offer more than a translation of the European term.

There is more change when one goes inside. The standards of comfort may rise no higher than you would expect at a cheap hotel in Lyons, but the route to Kashgar is not the penitential pilgrimage it was even as recently as three years ago. You will find fresh linen on the beds, a jug of water in each room (disinfectant tablets of course are a wise precaution) and generally one person who understands simple English.

But tolerable as the journey may now be, and however astonishing the landscape, the main purpose of the expedition is to see Kashgar and its Sunday market. This is the westernmost town in China, and in the last century it was the place where agents of the Russian and British empires put their ears to the dragon's heartbeat and to each other, sending back memos that must have taken weeks to get to St. Petersburg and Whitehall. The old consulates are still there, disregarded and crumbling under vines. There is also a mosque to be seen, by those who will.

But you go for the market, held under hempen awnings that lap at the wind in the wide blue of the sky. Fat ocher melons tumble from carts. Piles of walnuts are scorchingly surveyed by women whose faces have taken on the same texture. Traders in carpets sit smoking Russian cigarettes, and flicking ash onto the rich crimson. Others wait behind ranks of copper pans, bright orange-pink like parts of shellfish.

A boy with untoward calm holds forward a tray of oranges. A girl rides by with all the portions of a pig sisal-bound to her motorcycle. Young men call from stalls piled with junk for an audience to hear their tales of Persian glazed tiles, raw emeralds, patches of needlework and Alexandrian coins. Here in an acre is the world.

Caveat, as they say, emptor. But I shall treasure the dish of celadon ware I picked up for the price of a taxi from Paddington to Victoria, and the memory of a sweet almond cake eaten under a mulberry tree at the place where China begins and ends.

Our correspondent travelled with Viaggi Polo Ltd, Ayas Acre, W1 (01-271-1292). Seven-day expeditions are priced from £849.

XXVI

in which there is yet another

interruption

"You must begin," said the master painter, "with imitation."

"Do you mean," she said quickly, unable to check herself from using more breath than was necessary, gasping from the embarrassment even she might have felt at this early stage of her apprenticeship, in a studio where otherwise they were boys and men who sat at desks by high windows, "the imitation of nature? For I think I showed you, before you were gracious enough to accept me as your pupil," and at the rise of an eyebrow she stumbled, then went on: "I mean, before I was admitted here, when you were examining my work, I think I showed you, or at least you saw, some studies I had made for my former teacher, studies of flowers, waterfalls, I think there were some of trees, and a theater, I distinctly remember a theater, with so many figures in the stockade, and an old man conversing with a youth . . ."

"You will know," he began severely, before relaxing to a lower and warmer tone, "that the imitation of nature is reserved for great and wise talents. Theirs is the second level of perfection. Those at the first level, the greatest and wisest, imitate nothing, but instead accomplish the creation of what has not been in the world until their realization of it. But we must begin at the third level, which is that of the imitation of art. I think you are ready for this challenge: your studies whispered as much to me, whatever their other noises, which we must try to render into silence."

They had been standing close to the door: an adieu had perhaps been prepared before the master's first words, and indeed the pupil was carrying her brushes in a long-strapped linen bag dangling almost to the ground from her left hand, and she was waiting as if to go, showing her back, with the master facing her and also facing the row of other students to the right, each face turned a little from its white paper-screened window to observe the dialogue. But then she herself turned a little, into the studio again, her eyes presumably following the master as he strode to a tall teak cupboard on his dais and removed a box, a box covered with paper that had an exuberant tracery of vegetal design in vivid green on a white ground. She raised her right hand to receive it.

"Here. Let this be your model. Call me to your studio when your work is completed."

So she took the box to her studio, and drew off the lid, which came stiffly, with a stuttering scrape of cardboard on cardboard, and found inside a scroll, which she carefully withdrew as if it might fall apart at a rough gesture, and unrolled on the plain pine table before her. The scroll had perhaps not been surveyed in many years: it wanted, like a disturbed caterpillar, like a caterpillar which has been asked a terrifying question, to return to the safety of coiling. But she held the silk-backed paper with a slightly spread hand at each side, and stopped its bashful impulse at a stage where rolled cornets formed at the four corners of a sheet that was perhaps four feet wide and eighteen inches deep. Then she looked, or rather continued to look, for astonishment and intense inspection had begun with her first glimpse of the picture.

It was a fête champêtre of the Tang dynasty, a scene of the utmost civility and liveliness. To the left, almost brushed by her thumb, for the margins were narrow, was a teahouse, seen in oblique perspective so that the front of the building rose and receded as the viewing eye traveled rightward. This teahouse was a wooden building of simple design, with steps on the left (that is, facing out from the picture) up to a veranda that went the length of the façade, and with enclosed quarters behind (that is, to the left). Ladies in gowns of superb color—peacock blue, tangerine, ultramarine—were stationed on the steps, seeming to wait there, though very possibly some were passing as they went on errands into and out from the interior; indeed, a few were carrying trays, or pots, or baskets. Other figures, in jackets of sapphire and vermilion, were lolling out through windows, cups poised in their hands. Then in front of the building, or to the right in the picture, was a low fence of a single wooden rail reaching from one squat square post to another, and one might imagine that the fence completely encircled, or rather enrectangled, the teahouse, except for a single break in the middle of its front length to admit entrances and exists. And some figures were indeed moving, or placed as if they were moving, toward or away from this aperture, in both directions, while others sat on the unpainted white within the enclosure, which extended almost to the center point of the scene.

The other half was similarly thronged. There was a small

circle of women sitting with their legs pushed out in front of them, or reclining on an elbow, their gowns, in prescribed folds, outlined in black against the whiteness, so that they might have seemed to be floating on a cloud were it not that their postures intimated gravity. A man with a topknot was seated looking away from them, his back arched forward in the substantial, purposeful curve of a musical instrument, his hands clasped around his tightly folded knees. Some children, their heads excessively large and spherical, were running in an uneven line at the front, toward the teahouse. A man with parallel lines of beard and an oyster cloak was leaning rightward on a black stick, while the tall black fin of his headdress reared in the opposite direction toward the widening curl of its finial. And facing him, perhaps listening to some story, looking upward perhaps only because he had been drawn smaller as being of lesser importance, was a much younger man, hatless. Servants, as one would have supposed them to be, stood bearing lanterns on long canes, or perhaps slowly walked, emerging from the copse of drooping willows at the right edge, toward the back. And from those clumped bells of tremulous striations there came also a horizontal line that marked the river bank, taking the eye back along to the knobbed roof of the teahouse, past the round-topped triangles, striped like geodes in section, that stood for mountains, past the sky clamant with characters and flying with the impressions of seals in black and cinnabar.

She raised her head from the view and sighed deeply, no doubt in wonderment at the liveliness and civility of the scene, but no doubt too in mingled fear and excitement at the magnitude of the task that the picture dumbly commanded. One might wonder if the master had chosen this particular scroll as best fitted to bring out the pupil's skills, or to challenge her acquiring of new ones, or whether his choice had been made at random, whether perhaps he might even have been ignorant of what was contained within the box he thrust into his pupil's waiting hand.

However, she set to work at once, and wiped the dust from four lead weights of various sizes, which she placed on the corners of the outstretched scroll. Then she fetched from a shelf some papers of similar quality, and compared them closely with the painting, eyes flashing from the finished work to the virginal candidate under inspection, until she found a piece that matched in color, weave and weight what the original artist had used. Then with a rule and a point of silver she measured the painting and cut her paper accordingly; and then again with the rule and the point of silver she noted the dimensions of the larger features, and plotted on her paper where the teahouse, fence, figures, trees, bank and mountains were to go. Satisfied with her work so far, and leaving on the table the pinioned picture and her own paper stippled with dots as with a fine shower of pepper, she went to her bed, for the paper was now beginning to turn gray more uniformly in the dimming light of that first day.

But many times the sun was to rise and set while the copy grew toward the original. Meanwhile she did not return to the master, but sought advice from her earlier teachers about so many things that troubled her. How had painters of the Tang obtained their vibrant scarlet, which covered the paper with thick color, obscuring the fibers, yet had the opulent mattness of the petal of a pelargonium? Were the black outlines of the teahouse's timbering to be set in place before or after the wash of brown? Was the malachite of Tachu available at this period? Would the tendrilous branches of the trees have been done with a pen or with a fine brush? Fortunately the artistic traditions of the Tang were well recorded and remembered, so that an ink-stained finger would be able to touch a reference in some treatise, or else tap at the table while thinking proceeded and then rise in the air with the realization that an answer was known.

And so the pupil gathered her information; though much

more came from the painting directly. She might need help from outside in matters of technique, but the welter of data was in front of her, awaiting only her observation: the picture was not only her model but also the system of instructions which told her how she might make her reproduction. She did not rush at obeying. Instead she measured and looked and compared with the most intimate attention while engaged on a roof cornice, or a pleat of drapery, or a branch, or a face. She was careful to imitate every stroke of pen or brush, to equal with precision every color, to follow the original even in its errors, as where a dab of kingfisher blue had been only roughly placed to coincide with the outline of the shirt of a boy fishing at the riverbank, or where the line between two planks extended beyond the edge of the teahouse roof. Such intensive work required the fullest concentration she could summon, and she was able to work for only an hour in the morning and a further hour in the afternoon, spending the rest of each day in reading, or in the composition of poems, or in lazing with her lover, or in indolent conversation, but never in painting or even sketching, for she was unable to proceed with any work of that kind while so much was being demanded by the Tang scene.

In future years she would feel, though with so much regret, that this had been the most difficult, the most absorbing and the most complete artistic work she had ever undertaken. And it seemed to her even while she was engaged on the work that her burden was so much heavier than that of the original artist, for he had been able to paint and draw with infinitely greater freedom. No doubt the picture was itself the reproduction of some view in his head, compounded perhaps of elements taken from life and of course from other paintings: his own, those of fellow artists of his period, and those of revered colleagues from the past. But in matters of detail he had been free. What did it matter if there were twenty-seven or twenty-eight branches limply cascading from the bole of a tree? What did it matter if the green of the robe of a lady at the teahouse steps were just a certain degree yellower than that of a boy's waving belt? What did it matter precisely where the topknot man was seated? Indeed, might he not be replaced, without damage to the composition, by a tub of chrysanthemums, or by a girl ceremoniously raising one leg, as in a dance? And it occurred to her that her knowledge of the painting was incommensurably greater than that of the original artist, because she was obliged to measure and consider and prepare every action she made at the paper, doing so with reference to what he had done unfetteredly. And sometimes from this she would conclude—especially toward the end of her work, when pride in her achievement was becoming intolerably hard to strangle—that her copy meant immeasurably more than the original, because purpose was drawn into the paper in every detail, because nothing was done unless at the end of a long process of deliberation. But then she considered that all her effort of will was directed toward its own extinction, since the measure of her success was the exactness with which her copy resembled something that had been created so much more freely, and by another.

Finally one morning the painting was finished, and she stood back to look at her table with the same wonderment as weeks before, but now with mingled relief and melancholy that the work had been completed. Of course, the copy was not quite identical with the original, despite all her pains. If she looked from one to the other with the most scrupulous inspection, then she could see where a line of hers might be thinner at some point than a line of his, because her brush had carried less ink, or been finer, or moved more swiftly. Or the texture of a washed area might be different because of some dissimilarity in the congregation of paper fibres. Or a portion of black might have less luster because it had dried more quickly.

These differences, however, she reasonably judged to be insignificant: the picture was ready for the later stages of its preparation as a simulacrum, and she called in first an engraver of seals to examine the prints which the artist and subsequent owners of the painting had placed like kites on his work, bearing monograms or in some cases more considerable inscriptions. Copies of the seals were duly prepared without error, sealmakers being used to fine work in a mirror world; and inks of matching black and cinnabar were compounded. Then, with judicious care and due measurement, and with all possible allowances for the variations in ink density that had in the original case been so arbitrarily permitted across each seal, the impressions were made.

And it seemed to the pupil that this was a point of crucial coincidence between original and copy, for the imprinting of a seal is a mechanical action done always in the same way, the square or circular block of stone being pressed between thumb and forefinger and rocked on the paper, so that here her hand was in the same flow as his had been so long before, whereas who can say with what movements he had darted and peered with his brushes and pens? Also there was the collusion of speed. While painting she had been moving so much more slowly than he, whereas now she felt herself to be reproducing not only his work but also his physical activity as he created that work, her nerves and muscles operating to the same purpose and with the same accord. Further, there was the agreement in risk. A misplaced seal (though that was unlikely given the precision of the anticipatory measurement), or an excess or underfill of ink (though all efforts had been made), or a smudge (though accident had been as far as possible excluded), would cause for either of them far graver damage than the occasional slip of pen or brush: an inappropriate or unlovely impression might have to be scraped off, and the worrying of the paper would be difficult to repair, disfiguring perfection whether of original or copy.

But against this rapture of closeness there was the poignancy of deliberate imperfections. Several of the seal prints on the original, it was obvious, could have been better performed: a red rectangle with two characters excised in white was poorly inked at the bottom left corner, and a large black square conveying perhaps a whole poem had been slightly swiveled clockwise in the pressing. The pupil was tempted to right these mistakes, for though she felt that apparent misjudgments or carelessnesses in the actual painting might have artistic value, there seemed no reason to find a purpose or a point in some failing of a mechanical process. And yet she refused to effect any improvement, but placed the impressions as exactly as possible in the way they had been placed before. And her tact was rewarded. No scraping away of fault was necessary, and she stood back to look at the seal marks. Of course, the copy was not quite identical with the original, despite all her pains. If she looked from one to the other with the most scrupulous inspection, then she could detect slight differences in the inking of seals, or in the uptake of ink by the paper fibers, or in the patterns of tiny round white shadows left by bubbles.

These differences, however, she reasonably judged to be insignificant: the picture was ready for the last stages of its preparation as a simulacrum, and she went to a merchant for silk on which to mount it, finding a piece that might have been cut from the same cloth that had served the Tang artist: it needed only to be rubbed with dust and to have two ovoid stains applied (chicken fat seemed an appropriate material, carefully dripped and encouraged into the right configuratrions). It was perhaps at this point that she wondered whether the master had intended her to go so far in copying the painting; but she knew she must. She had a woodcarver reproduce the twin poles of ebony to which the original painting was bound, and then she gummed the copy to the silk and fastened the silk to the poles, adding a tie of brown silk ribbon identical with the original's once it had been zealously thumbed a while.

But she left to the end what might have been the most difficult part of her task: imitating the characters. For the essence of calligraphy is in its speed, and the lettering of the Tang artist bore witness to his quick virtuosity, telling not only of the painting in the flourishes of its poetry but also of the artist's agile touch and swoop. The pupil knew that if she were to rival his speed, then her penmanship would easily reveal her handiwork, not because her characters would necessarily be inferior, but because they would have her style. On the other hand, to copy the original placing and shape of each stroke would require slow labor, and it would be exceedingly hard to catch the dash of the artist's script at so much lesser a pace. Perhaps it was because of these quandaries that she had kept the calligraphy till last, but eventually she decided that she would have to make her imitation in slow motion, yet make it so carefully that she reproduced the full substance of energy and life that was present in the original. So she proceeded, and after two weeks of the most painstaking work, more painstaking even than the effort of copying the painting had been, the superscription was complete. She stood back. Of course, the copy was not quite identical with the original, despite all her pains. If she looked from one to the other with the most scrupulous inspection, then she could spot how the ink spread differently in the filaments of the paper at one point, or how the exact contour of the arch at the top of one stroke was not quite in agreement, or how the ink of a horizontal bar was grainier.

These differences, however, she reasonably judged to be insignificant. All that remained was to complete the aging of the copy with a splash of tea, some scuffing at the lower edge, a wafting of ash to tone down in places the brilliance, and the odd tuck, crease or fold. Then she rolled her scroll tightly, until it imitated even the caterpillar shyness of the original. Finally she hung the two paintings side by side on the wall of her studio. They were identical. But no: one of the original's ebony poles had an incision that neither she nor the woodcarver had noticed before; it was carefully reproduced on the fellow. Now they were indeed identical, except in such insignificant discrepancies as she had noted, and though she had expected to feel elated at this point, still the elation was mingled with sadness and even foreboding. But she sent for the master.

The next morning he arrived, and without saying a word walked through her house and out into the garden, where she had her studio. He stood for many minutes looking at the two paintings, examining now one and then the other, or flipping his eyes from one to the other, or standing back to look at both together, or craning near to stare at some detail. And then he turned and smiled broadly at his pupil, who had been lingering close to the doorway.

"Many congratulations! Your success has been so complete that I am afraid you will have to tell me which is the original and which your copy. For even though this is a great and famous work, one which I have studied through many years, still you have reproduced it in every detail."

And then she realized: she had forgotten which was which. She looked at the two paintings. She thought hers must be the one on the right, but then she thought no, it must be the one on the left. But she would look stupid or worse if she hesitated, and so she said: "The one on the left is the work of the Tang painter, that on the right my copy."

"Then," he said, "I will take the original back with me. Again, many congratulations."

She must stop him. "No," she said. "Could I keep it for one more day after so long? I have spent so much time in examining its proportions, materials and techniques, but I have yet to make acquaintance with its essence."

The master looked at the two paintings. "You are right," he said. "The great work has an indefinable aura that no imitation, even one as excellent as your own, can quite recapture." He smiled and was gone.

Immediately after a farewell at the street the pupil rushed back to the two paintings. She looked at places where she knew there was a difference: in the texture of a wash, or the inking of a seal print, or the shape of the top of a calligraphic stroke. But in no case could she remember with certainty which author was indicated by the difference. Sometimes, and with blissful gratitude, she would feel confident that she had found some feature which unmistakeably was hers. But then, and with re-newed agitation, she would find on the same painting something she knew was the great artist's. What should she do? If by mistake she returned the copy to the master, then an important painting would henceforth be known only in an imitation made centuries later, while the original lay unregarded as a journey-man's travail. Perhaps the best course, she considered, would be to destroy one of the paintings; but then there was an even chance that a great work of the Tang would be lost forever. Or perhaps she should go to the master and admit what had hap-pened, but this idea she did not long entertain, for it would not only make her look foolish but also place the master in an awkward situation: he had asserted that the difference was evi-dent; he would either have to admit that this was not so, or else himself make a judgment that would certainly be a matter of chance, for she was convinced that if she could not tell the two paintings apart, after so many weeks of working with them, then decidedly he could not, for all his years of study. She looked again at the two paintings. One of them ought to resound with centuries and greatness; the other should be loud with the noise of her own strains and efforts. Both were silent. She retired to her bedchamber, and the next morning tossed a coin, which as it spun in the air, catching gold on its revolving rim in the rising sun, decided whether the original or the facsimile was returned to the master.

XXVII

in which I read more, of food

They had always told me that nothing new had happened in
Chinese cooking since the Shang empire, which was fine by me,
though in some moods I might have put the terminus post quem
at the opening of the Chagan-nur in Genoa Street. But that, with
its emphasis on the hardy cuisine of the northern slopes of the
Himalayas, was a special case, as distant from your standard
chop-suey house as L'Estragon Bleu is from the "French" restaurants of somewhere like Milton Keynes. One does not expect
repeat miracles.

So I went to Polo Po Lo with small enthusiasm. Nor was my
eagerness overmuch increased by the decor: one enters a diagonally transected box of grey and azure, and feels one has walked
into a ream of designer stationery. The Muzak is in the same

taste: Gregorian chant folding into sounds of trickling water. Despite recommendations from more than a few usually reliable sources, I was prepared to beat it.

But you have to be patient. You might have already noticed by this point in the evening's entertainment that the little man who bowed you to your table was not a Hong Kong Chinese but a native of Milan, and that the elephant-size piece of thin grey card that you hold in your hands, and that flops lubriciously toward your partner, macaronizes Cantonese and Italian. Personally I could do without such mongrels as Ta Liu Tei Li digging me in the spare ribs, but the effort to combine Chinese omnivorousness with Italian style is interesting and admirable. And the constructivist cane chairs, by Bauhaus out of Oxfam, are less offensive once you are seated in them.

I began with a risotto of smoked duck and ginger that contrived to be dry and fatty at the same time, however pretty it looked with its petticoat of radicchio peeping out. The Foo Yung Parmigiana—scrambled egg with the merest scrape of cheese—was a better bet, or you could try a plate of vegetables steeped in rice wine vinegar. I have also heard the odd eulogy or two for the Brodo Maffeo, confected from chicken, noodles, coriander and star-shaped slices of baby carrot. But the grey fish soup, dotted with intricately cut patches of red and yellow peppers, is probably best avoided except by those who have a fancy to eat a Miró.

The main dishes mostly feature chicken or veal, which made me a shade desperate, if not enough to fling me into the arms of the Calamari Foochow, which promised a sauce of ink, mushroom ketchup and bitter chocolate. Pollo Kublai Khan proved a much safer choice, with steaming, subtly anis-scented slices of breast meat impeccably presented on a divan of golden saffron noodles, with tiny onions and spheres of a stiff spinach purée in attendance.

The escalope offerings include a nice little number with raspberries and long black-stained burdock roots among its accouterments, as well as something fearsomely borne in while still spluttering in argument with chopped leek and pink marbled beans. Apart from these woody last, ingredients tasted fresh, and obviously somebody in the kitchen knows how to order spices in small enough quantities that they stand some chance of being intercepted at their best. Only the sweet and sour sauce on an unlucky clutch of prawns had some odour of the bottle.

Puddings in Chinese restaurants are generally a no-go area, but here the Italian influence has contrived some gaiety. There are perky little rice cakes studded with crystallized peas, and the gelati are as good as you could expect, particularly one flavored with citron and sandalwood. The house also has its own version of zabaglione done with Chinese brandy, though no doubt still tasting like invalid food.

The wines are mostly inferior Italian and overpriced. I drank a delightfully fragrant and pale tea throughout, though Chinese beers are also available. Expect to pay £40 a head, or £50 with wine.

Polo Po Lo. Kerman Court, WC2 (01-271-1292). Open noon–2 pm Mon to Fri and 7–11.30 pm Mon to Sat.

XXVIII

in which he tells me
of the third of five visits
to places of interest in Peking

~~~~~~

So once more the springtime walk through the dry detritus of
the previous fall, which made no mark on our white slippers but
billowed at each step in soft, slow waves of dust and square
particles, rising into the air and again gently settling. I knew
better than to enquire as to our destination: questions of such
a sort were left unanswered, when they were not blocked by
some sly misunderstanding, philosophy or paradox. We walked
on in silence, of which we always had sufficient, until it seemed
that we reached the place, for we turned a corner in the path and
had before us the prospect of a great white beehive of a building,
with smooth walls that scooped up and flattened toward a point,
and with small square windows set irregularly. There was a door,
in the middle of the building as we approached, but placed at

what appeared to be first-floor level, to be reached by a ladder of rope and wooden rungs. This seemed an unnecessary inconvenience, so unnecessary as to embolden me to say as much to the Failed Sage, while holding the ladder so that he could make the first ascent.

"Would you rather there were no ladder, and therefore no possibility of entrance or exit?"

"Why no," I said, "for then the building would be totally useless."

"Perhaps not, if those within never wished to leave, and those without never wished to see inside. But the point of the ladder is surely," and he said this as if it were something he had not considered before and was not entirely convinced about, "to oblige us to notice leavings and enterings. The point is not the difficulty. The point is the point made by the difficulty."

By this time he was up, standing on a small platform and holding a rail to the right of the door. Unsteadily I followed, and when I too had reached the platform he opened the door for us to go in.

There were white rush mats on the floor, dim passages to right and left, and another corridor leading ahead to the center of the building, where it later appeared there was a spiral staircase lit by a hole in the conical roof. For the moment we took the passageway to the left, which gave into a chamber, still rush-matted, where an old man sat scanning a scroll: scanning and then putting the thing down on his lap with a clatter while his eyes turned to peer straight ahead (though not at us), then scanning again and, as I presumed, pondering again, scanning and pondering in what seemed to me a regular rhythm, as if his movements had been set to the machinery of some enormous pendulum. We observed him through perhaps six or seven cycles of his inspection and wondering, which he continued as if we were not there. Then we passed to other chambers, in each of which the same scene was disclosed of an old man reading and pausing, reading and pausing, though each at his own speed of cogitation, so that I had the impression of being inside some great timepiece, seeing wheels that itched at different rates, though all, it was tempting to suppose, related, all working to a common purpose. Eventually, after we had stood for different intervals before perhaps six or seven of these studying and considering scholars (for such I had taken them to be), my condition of ignorance and perplexity had built up the power to carry me through another question, and I asked my companion if this might be another of the city's libraries.

"In a sense," he said, "it is the most abstracted of our libraries, for what is of concern here is not knowledge but the knowledge of knowledge. And yet in a sense too it is the most practical, for it is here that knowledge touches the world most intimately. Those that you see at work here are our knowledge guardians. Any discovery or invention, in whatever field, is submitted to them for approval as a legitimate addition to public knowledge. Every morning a messenger arrives, to bring new material for inspection, and to take away what has been dealt with."

"But how," I said, "do the guardians decide on legitimacy? Do they consult other documents, perform tests . . . ?"

"By no means. The only aid they require is their experience: you will have noticed that the guardians are old." Indeed, most of them wore their hair in long gray curls over their scarlet gowns. "They are not appointed to this place until they have served a long time in another capacity."

"Do you mean," I said, "that their venerable age permits them to decide whether something is true or not just by thinking about it?" I suppose, in retrospect, that I must have sounded doubtful, even to a degree scornful.

"Not at all: you misunderstand. The truth of what is brought here has already been established by relevant experts. What is at issue now is not whether these things are true, but whether they may be known. The guardians may give any of three judgments: that something is fit to be known, that it is not fit to be known, or that it is fit to be surmised. Anything placed in this last category may be resubmitted after perhaps a few years, while things deemed fit to be known then take their places in public libraries, school curricula, and so forth."

"What of those things thought unfit?"

"Not 'unfit,' just not fit: there is a difference. But as you may imagine, this is by far the largest category. Very few things gain even the moderate and tentative public circulation of things fit to be surmised; additions to the body of knowledge fit to be known are exceedingly rare. By far the majority of discoveries and inventions are pronounced not fit to be known, and restricted to scholarly libraries."

"And may they too be resubmitted after some time?"

"It would seem unlikely," he said. "We must suppose that damnation in these cases is eternal."

"But why should anything that is true not be fit to be known?"

"I would rather ask: why should people be confused by having their suppositions extended or replaced, especially when each extension or replacement is only a step toward the next?"

"Because they are thereby brought closer to the truth."

"To the truth, or away from it? We should rather keep the truth we know."

"But truth is not fixed," I said. "It is perpetually to be sought: one might even say that truth is a journey and not a destination."

"Yet that would seem to produce a highly unstable situation." We spoke still stayed on the central staircase. "What if your search for new truth were to lead you to truths that are unbearable, or that would undermine your self-esteem, or that could not be adequately controlled? These are matters where the utmost caution is needed: hence our knowledge guardians.

"But they must speak for themselves," he went on. "You will

find that each is a specialist in a particular branch of knowledge. Hear them."

And the guardian of poetry said: "Mine is beyond doubt the most difficult task, because great quantities of poetry are of course constantly being written, while only very little can be passed as fit to be known. There is, after all, a limit to the amount of poetry that can be useful, and it happens only very seldom that a poet will treat a theme more successfully than it was treated by one of the great masters of our anthologies. In such cases the new poem will be substituted; but it is, as I say, a very rare occurrence. I can recollect just two poems that I have approved. Out of how many? No doubt two hundred a day throughout a period of twenty years. The calculation is beyond me: let me introduce you to my colleague."

And the guardian of mathematics said: "Mine is beyond doubt the most difficult task, because mathematics is not a subject in which old knowledge can be displaced when new is added: the elements are all linked, as strings in a net. So if I pass something, there is an addition to the store of knowledge. That is something we try to avoid. I therefore have to be more scrupulous than most of my fellow guardians. Indeed, so far I have not found it possible to admit any growth in our mathematical knowledge, though I could mention many things that have passed before these eyes: negative numbers, differential calculus, the theory of sets . . . all regrettably impermissible. How long have I been here? You must excuse me, my memory is poor in such matters: let me introduce you to my colleague."

And the guardian of history said: "Mine is beyond doubt the most difficult task, because things keep happening. Moreover, history lies under threat of extension at its further end, for the labors of archaeologists and archivists, however much we try to restrain these unruly disciplines, constantly present us with new facts to be either accommodated or rejected. I could say also that history is the mother of all knowledge, for all knowledge is knowledge of what is known, and therefore of what was, not what is. However, I try to keep my purview to the doings of emperors, the engagement of battles, the building of cities, and such like. It is in all conscience enough. And on those rare occasions when I judge an event fit to be known, then something from the record of the past has to be deleted or conflated, for we know that the memory is a delicate faculty and cannot deal with too much information. Do I concern myself with the histories of other people? The question has, I think, seldom arisen, but let me introduce you to my colleague."

And the guardian of geography said: "Mine is beyond doubt the most difficult task, because only very infrequently does new information reach me; and so, since we cannot be idle, I am obliged to spend many days, even weeks, sometimes months, in considering whether we should know of a small island in the great eastern ocean, or of a port where ivory, gold and salt fish may be had, or of a yellow-haired tribe in the distant west. You see, it is very clear to us that curiosity about other regions would bring needless disturbance to the corpus of approved knowledge, and therefore few embark on journeys of exploration or listen to strangers' tales. You may have noticed this."

There were others to be heard before we descended the rope ladder, and walked away, and continued our conversation, while ahead of us the messenger ran with his two sheaves of scrolls.

"Presumably," I said, "he will take these to some library for their incarceration, or for their more or less modest distribution."

"Perhaps that is what the guardians imagine," he said. "Who can tell? Certainly they are somewhat rarefied spirits, by reason of their long specialization and devotion to judgment, both encouraging an aloofness from the actual. But in fact the scrolls will go now to another place, so that the decisions of these guardians may be compared with those of others; for you must know that we have many such academies of guardians, and many such houses of consideration. Then a final—or at least we may suppose it to be final—judgment will be made by the guardians of guardians."

The messenger by now was out of sight.

XXIX

in which we cross a desert

"But" (and I hear his words again, in my head as I write, the sentence circling in repetition or crisscrossing through fragments, idling as the voice waits for my pen to catch up with it) "the deserts were important." (We are, of course, back there in our cell. It must surely be many weeks now. I'm probably beginning to wonder if there is anywhere else in the world. Or rather I should say I *was* probably beginning to wonder. My present circumstances are very different.)

"Look" (that word at least I can recall with certainty: I feel it in my throat, catching), I said. "We have had one desert already. To my mind it wasn't the most" (I think I probably searched for an adjective: there might have been a slight pause indicating as much) "successful episode, but that's neither here nor there." (On second thoughts, or whatever, I don't dislike it so much. These things change. And perhaps I was just being rhetorical.) "The point is" (do I see my finger stab at the table?) "that deserts have their limitations. I'm not blaming you," (indeed I wasn't: that would've been grotesque, even by this stage) "but when you're out there on the sand we" (I think I was probably including you in this) "lose sight of you. It's" (I retracted my hands to my lap, the case being made) "inevitable."

"*You*" (I think he was probably not including you in this) "may lose sight of me, but that is precisely" (the bright sibilants I seem to see in the intensity of his stare) "the point" (or would he really have thrown my own word so swiftly back at me?). "In the desert" (I think he sat back) "one is visible only to oneself. In a very real sense" (hah!) "one is oneself only in the desert."

(And perhaps I felt brave enough, or outraged enough, to leap in with some such words as) "What" (yes, I believe I did) "nonsense!" (and yet I hope I didn't return his own self-righteous glare). "One exists" (the irony of our own situation wasn't lost on me, you may be sure) "only in relation to other people. Part of the measure of me" (I took a slurp from the jug: we had no other vessel, and had each learned to be tolerant of the other's spittle, as of the greenish color and dank taste of the water; sometimes I'd wonder if I could truly remember how clean water tasted, and would taste again) "is the extent to which" (but now I can't remember what the taste I imagined was like, let alone whether it was accurate) "I'm not" (after all, it was a long time ago) "you. We're defined" (or perhaps this was something I said much later, to somebody else) "and indeed" (or something someone else said to me) "we define ourselves" (I feel it must have been) "by our" (one or the other) "society" (but let it stand). "Alone in the desert—"

"I was never alone!" (he rocked, sprang forward from the waist, and the impact of an elbow made the table shudder an inch across the flagstones). "You forget my father and uncle again" (indeed I do, and did, and now it's rather too late to introduce them). "Besides which," (and he sat back again) "there were our servants, a man as guide and interpreter, and nearly always, certainly if we were crossing a desert, other companies of travelers going in the same caravan."

"Indeed" (such a useful word for effectively closing an argument, or indeed beginning one). "But we stray from our way, like those desert travelers who hear strange spirits in the wind and are parted from their companions" (I can't now remember if this was something he'd mentioned: it'd be useful in any event).

"I" (this was his voice of hauteur, recognizable even in a single sound: I knew its disparagement well enough) "never heard such" (the calculated gap) "fairy stories when I was in the deserts of Persia and China" (perhaps then the story wasn't his; I've heard enough). "But I dare say they occur to fill up" (and again the hesitation) "vacancies in the minds of some."

"My point" (I was being reasonable, having learned to ignore this supercilious tone, which I sensed he disliked in himself, and disliked me the more for eliciting) "is rather as you're admitting, that nothing happens in the desert. We have the sand, the clear sky, the early morning reveille, the waiting animals, the wind, the view, the caravanserai, the colorful hosts. We've done it once." (I leave you to find the place.) "Do we have to do it again? Besides, this Lop, this Desert of Lop: it invites ridicule. And ridicule" (I felt a touch of professional formality wouldn't come amiss) "in that it takes the reader out from the book, is the enemy of literary success."

"Are we then to aim" (he stopped while he scraped the jug across the table and put it to his own lips, then set it down again) "to aim for success now that we have abandoned truth?" (He got up from the table and turned around to look at the candle on the sideboard, showing me his back.) "Abyss upon abyss" (the words trembled in the candlelight as his breath reached the flame. But then he suddenly spun back to face me, as if he'd been reminded of something). "Let me tell you a story" (I took up my pen: here was water in the desert after all).

"In traversing the desert we came upon a dried-up river bed, and in the middle of what one might have imagined to be in the summer the muddy floor of a gushing stream, haunt of hydra and the mayfly larva, right in the middle of this desiccated water-course there was a crack, perhaps only an inch across, but perhaps many miles long, for it bisected this echo or shadow or imprint of a river as far as the eye could see, in both directions. And an old Uighur told me that a great devil had once passed this way, when the land was rich and green, and had tried to sodomize the local shaman, but had been defeated by the power of an amulet, and had slaked his lust then in the river, which had boiled, and whose bed had then split, so that the water fell through and scoured out a passage at a lower level. And the Uighur said that if I put my ear to the crack I would hear the water flowing beneath. Of course I did so, and indeed there was a sound of rushing water to be heard. But I thought this must be the effect of the wind blowing over the opening, and told him so, at which he merely shrugged and walked on, walked into the morning sun as I watched him from where I still lay prone in the disputed river bed. And because it had not mattered to him that I had not believed his story, I felt suddenly inclined to take it as fact. And yet that would have required me to believe in devils who went about craving the parched arses of wild priests and then taking revenge on rivers for their rejection. Nevertheless, I took from my pocket a long strand of cotton thread, tied a small pebble to one end, and slowly lowered the apparatus down through the crack. It accepted many feet of my line (I began to wonder at the anatomy of demons, and to think the shaman's escape had been even luckier than I had supposed), until I felt the downward tug joined by another, in the direction of the erstwhile river. I quickly pulled up the string. The pebble was glistening and wet to the touch. Or it was bone dry. Or I never made the test. Or it was not a devil but an emperor whose potency astonished nature. Or it was a young maiden who allured and repulsed him. Or it was a boy, a beautiful boy with one testicle much larger than the other. Or there was no Uighur and I have invented the whole story." (Or I have.)

XXX

in which we hear a dispute
concerning a chapter missing
from the present recension

——Take this matter of the salamander. It's not an animal, says
our author, for no animal could live in flames. It's a stone:
asbestos. This is reason parting itself from fantasy, resplend-
ently: I'd see the image of the asbestos cloth, glowing white in
the fire, as the emblem of that parting, that victory. And he
provides exactly the evidence we'd want. He's heard the full
story from his Turkish companion, Zurficar, who we're informed
spent three years in the mineral industry at Ghinghintalas. He's
also seen the true facts for himself. He even directs us to tangible
proof: the asbestos cloth taken back to Rome as a gift from
Kublai Khan to the pope.
——But doesn't his insistence speak against him? Three times
he tells us: these are the true facts; believe me; everything else

is falsehood. He sounds like an advertisement. Why the hell should we trust him?

——Because he's not talking to us. You have to understand he was writing for people who'd thoroughly accepted the idea of flame-born reptiles.

——Just as he thoroughly accepts other nonsense. You've only to look at the episodes that surround this one. Several pages are given over to stuff about Prester John, with all kinds of circumstantial details about the tribute the Mongols paid him, about Genghis Khan's wooing of his daughter, about the battle at which he was defeated by Genghis. There's even direct speech attributed to him, to this phantom!

——But you forget the hand of the ghost writer. The Prester John material was clearly inserted as a piece of conventional romance: it uses all the same formulae.

——I wish I had your facility in distinguishing report from fabrication. Suppose Chinese archaeologists were to discover the tomb of Prester John, bedecked with Christian inscriptions and an obliging inscription recording that he was indeed killed in battle by Genghis Khan in 1200. Would that change your view of the text?

——Yes, of course: it'd be a delayed vindication of the author.

——Then it's just as I supposed. You accept or reject what he says according to your own criteria. You accept the asbestos because it accords with your own version of reality; you reject Prester John because he doesn't. You have the author journeying through a landscape that's your own.

——No, because we live in the same world. If Prester John now is proved to be a historical figure, then so he was for our author.

——Not so: then he was a myth.

——But perhaps not for our author, who may have had reliable information.

——He gives no evidence of that.

———But at least he had the concept of evidence, of proof, of empirical reality. The asbestos episode shows as much. Of course, these were early days: a great deal even of his own age was hidden from him. I see the two of them working away in their Genoese prison, perhaps by night, while the sun flashes on a spear an aborigine has launched at a squatting kangaroo, while an Aztec priest checks the calculations of the coming solar eclipse, while a family in Zimbabwe sleep, their bellies filled for the first time in a fortnight, while a child is born on the banks of the Orinoco, while an Eskimo woman, lungs swarming with things that would go unnamed through many generations, dies. I grieve for the ignorance of our authors.

———But in doing so you posit a world that wasn't theirs. You interpose your mind into their time, where it has no place. You speak as if the past had the reality of another country, as if there is notionally a place called 1298 to be visited and inspected. But the existence of their time is only in their records, such as this. We shouldn't regret our authors' ignorance of a world that only we imagine: we should rather regret our ignorance of what really was the imagined world they inhabited. I see a world in which the roc and the wyvern have as much validity as the common crow, in which the orbits of the planets are the dwellings of angels, in which heaven and hell appear on the maps. I grieve for the ignorance of ourselves.

XXXI

in which I read yet more, of a room

Princess Maria Barbara degli Poli ("call me Bobbie") spends most of her time in the study of her third-floor apartment, "high enough to feel oneself belonging to the canal without having to endure its odor." With her husband, brother-in-law and son so often traveling on business, she is the lynchpin of the family commercial and business empire. As she explains, somebody has to stay at the center of the wheel, and the deceptively slim Olivetti computer to the left of her seventeenth-century Spanish walnut desk puts her in instant contact with the firm's offices throughout the world. Many an agent must spend anxious hours waiting for the next enquiry to flash on the monitor in imperious green under command from the princess's fingers. But does she mind being left on her own so much?

"You know, I had a very lonely childhood. My parents were in the diplomatic service, and I was brought up by a succession of middle-aged French ladies who kept falling into declines on account of the climate here. You know how it is. Like any only child, I was grossly overindulged and at the same time neglected. I learned to make my own amusement, and to gain control, I would say, of my own resources. And now I rather like being by myself.

"I never take a holiday, except sometimes perhaps for a little skiing. As I say, somebody has to mind the shop, and I think I have no regrets. When I think of my husband and my son, and of course my brother-in-law, out there in China or the Middle East, then I just thank God that I am here within reach of the necessities of life: mineral water, La Fenice, and good plumbing, in that order."

And yet, I suggest, she must miss her family when they are away so much. "Don't you believe it. I always say that a husband and wife should see each other for six weeks in the year. Maximum! Of course, when you are young, then it is a little different. Maybe then you could manage ten weeks.

"But seriously, I am surrounded by my husband. If ever I am missing him, I have only to pick up one of these beautiful things and he is with me." Her weightily bangled arm directs my gaze around the room. The majestic ebony fireplace to the left carries a rank of lesser trophies on its mantel: a small dark-chocolate-glazed dish from Nishapur, a gilt Nepalese Buddha with a wave of hair in tight curls, the ivory baton of a Chinese court official, a rosewood box inlaid with lapis lazuli and mother of pearl, a stuffed salamander.

To the right of the window is a bamboo painting on silk, bought in Canton for "ridiculously few dollars." The hunting scene on the opposite wall is a panel from an eighteenth-century Japanese screen. And in the center of the room a Balinese puppet in silk and brass stares at its reflection in a Mies van der Rohe table.

The princess is particularly fond of this item. "I had Alexander Calder make me a wire stand for my little Shiva, so that he would not have to sit there looking floppy and undignified. It's so cleverly done: look, you hardly see the support. That man had such a gift."

Others too have benefited from the princess's enlightened patronage of contemporary artists. "You know, I think it is so important, if you are somebody who loves beautiful things, that you should leave beautiful things behind you, you know, like a wake from a ship. And if you cannot create them yourself, if you have not the gift, then you have to help others to do so, no? And I have been very lucky in my artists, very lucky."

Yet there is no modern art in this room. "No, the reason for that is very simple. I could not work and be staring at a Jackson Pollock or an Arshile Gorky. You know, these things have a life: they breathe. They are not, not, not décor." The princess pronounces this last word with the utmost disdain. "So in here I have things that are beautiful and full of memories, but, if you like, dead in themselves."

One of the dove-gray telephones rings, a message appears on the computer screen, an assistant comes in with a letter to be signed, and the princess returns to her chieftainship of the family enterprise.

XXXII

in which I come to a great wall

I reach the halfway stage with some relief. Though in a sense it gets easier. For one thing, he's given up objecting. Maybe soon he'll even give up reading, though at the moment he sits there with three or four pages in his right hand and a left forefinger touched at his lips. Perhaps I've become more passive too, just accepting what he says, when he says it, whatever it is.

But I can't help feeling confused. For instance, by now he ought to have reached the Great Wall, or at least be somewhere near it. (I have to confess my grasp of his route is becoming ever hazier. You must forgive me.) He refers to plenty of place names—Tangut, Tenduc, Sin-chau, Kan-chau—but they're scattered points: I just try to find the line that makes the best fit, try to snake after him across the hills to the east.

Still, the wall's a puzzle (futile achievement as it was, Genghis Khan simply bribing the guards to let him through with his golden horde, and perhaps its most useful function being, then as now, to stem a little the wind from the north—not that one should altogether disregard a service to agriculture and comfort). How could he have missed it? Even if his journey took another route, he must've encountered it during his other travels when he was based in Peking. He must at least have heard about it. So why no mention?

Possibly for him it wasn't so extraordinary. Possibly he took it for granted. Living there for twenty years, almost in its shadow, he stopped noticing it, just as he stopped noticing all those other things he fails to mention: tea, the cooking, gunpowder, calligraphy (Rubrouck was so much keener an observer). Of course, I can supply all these and other things from my own knowledge: that's the advantage of collaborative work. But I can't see what he alone saw and doesn't or won't report. I look at those eyes, even now as they turn in tight slalom down the page, but I can't look into their memory. I come to a great wall.

XXXIII

in which I take my leave

(Beyond that wall I can't go. Let him be your guide into Peking, when and how he will. Addio.)

XXXIV

in which I attend a postmortem

The head, of course, was on a small table of its own, at the further end of the room. Which to me was some relief, since the trunk by itself seemed so much less human for having been robbed of its chief sign of individuality: it might almost have been a great taproot, or a species of mushroom, or something else vegetal slicked out from the sea. Or at least it might have been any of these things before the anatomist began to cut into the flesh along lines he had brushed in black ink across the chest of the corpse. His carving was expert, done with a bronze knife that moved with fluttering speed in his right hand, while with the middle and index fingers of his left he pressed and stretched the skin ahead, all the while holding his head still and back, the eyebrows arched, the eyes turned down in appraisal of his work as it happened. He was both student and examiner in his own discipline.

When the cutting was complete, when the bodily covering had been eased back by the two assistants, all but I formed their mouths into Os and made that throaty "orrrgh" I had heard so often in Peking at such moments of surprise and delight. I scanned the four faces of amazement—the anatomist, his assistants, the Failed Sage ("We shall be five," he said, possibly with a smile. "It is an auspicious number!")—but my thoughts were lagging with another who had missed this sight by a millennium. For it is recorded of the learned Galen that he knew others before him had been permitted the practice of anatomy on corpses, and no doubt it crossed his mind that this might be legally tolerable again, while he could trespass only within monkeys and pigs. What would he not have given to pass his eyes and fingers through these entrails!

With these thoughts in my mind, I asked my companion if human anatomy had always been permitted in Cathay.

"By no means," he said. "That extension of custom is something for which we have to thank our present master. Under the Sung, as under their predecessors, interference with cadavers was utterly proscribed. Our anatomists were obliged to pursue their studies by examining the bodies of children who had been ravaged by wolves, ever wary lest any attempt to enlarge a wound, turn back a flap of skin, pry within or encourage the extrusion of an organ were to be reported and deemed to have exceeded the bounds of propriety. But now there are no such restrictions and no such anxieties, except that only the corpses of those executed may be cut open. And there are always sufficient executions that this is not a serious disturbance to us."

After this exchange we turned to inspecting the feast of offal laid before us, the casket of globose, damp and soft jewels. I could recognise the liver from its similarity in color and texture to the livers of lambs and calves I had eaten during the journey and before; the kidneys too were familiar from the table and the butchery. And the slabs of pale sponge attached to a corrugated pipe must be the lungs, through which, as Galen says, the air of the outer world is brought into the heart of the being, as through the eyes it is brought into the head. But my slow and hesitant examination of the contents was coincident with another, quicker and dashing, which the anatomist executed, using his knife as spatula and pointer, speaking rapidly to tell us the clarities he saw in what was stumbling vagueness to us. My companion translated.

"The anatomist is demonstrating to his pupils what he describes as the five sensible organs, which, unless I mistake, you call the lungs, the liver, the heart, the kidneys and the bladder. These are associated with the five significant waters, which I think are rendered by your names of blood, phlegm, yellow bile, black bile and urine, and the five frequent passions, which I have more confidence in translating as anger, lust, laughter, melancholy and inspiration. They are further connected with the five objects of respect, which are parents, ancestors, the emperor, the gods and the earth, and with the five means of sensation, which are sight, hearing, savor, touch, and sexual conjunction. And all these fives are under the governance of the five planets, whose names in your language are, I regret, unknown to me."

"To me also," I said. "What little I know of astronomy I learned from a fork-bearded Arab in . . . Isfahan, I think it was, or it may have been Yazd."

"It does not matter," he said. "In my opinion these quincunxes are of an exceedingly speculative character. You will not find two anatomists who will agree about them: one will say that the stomach or intestines or brain must be counted among the sensible organs in place of the lungs or kidneys, another that semen or, if I have the name correctly, cerebrospinal fluid is to be included among the five significant waters, another that the five frequent passions are certainty, anxiety, loss, honor and embarrassment. And there are other anatomists who count the parts in sixes or sevens or fours. Very little in anatomy is agreed, which in my opinion makes it a considerably less satisfactory art than poetry."

While we talked the anatomist had proceeded from demonstration to the business of preparing specimens. Each of the five sensible organs, by his reckoning, was cut from its place and delivered to one of the assistants, who would weigh it, after which the second assistant would measure its dimensions and note down the figures.

"Presumably, though," I said as these tasks went on, "there is some general agreement about the function of the organs."

"Function?"

"Yes. I refer to their purpose within the body and their methods of operation. For instance, Galen teaches that the heart is a vessel which contracts in order to expel the blood into the furthest reaches of the body, and then expands so that it draws back the sanguineous tide."

"Some of our anatomists are of the same view. Others hold that the heart is the manufacturer or the cleanser of the blood, or that it maintains the blood in circulation through, as it were, a network of canals, or that it converts blood into air, or water, or thought. As I say, anatomy is a field rife with hypothesis, and because it is so new an art, the canons of accomplishment and appreciation are as yet unformed. You see our friends here weighing, measuring and sketching: they will no doubt go on to produce diagrams which may propose ingenious correlations with the shapes of the mountains of Huang Shan, or with the five colors of the rainbow, or with the festivals of our calendar, or with the crime for which the subject was executed, or with the disposition of his character. But I regret I find all this rather tedious."

"I confess I might as well," I said, trying to agree with my companion without injuring any pride he might feel even in this wayward and unfocused expression of his culture (for I was still so ignorant of where his pride lay). "But my question was about the purposes of the organs, which would seem surely to be the principle aim of anatomy to uncover."

"And why," he said, "should anatomy have an aim, any more than the organs of the body exist merely to fulfill some function?"

"Because there would be little point in doing it otherwise?"

"You judge by your own values. If a thing has no purpose you say that it is unworthy of consideration: is that not a kind of egoism? Moreover, if you make so much of purpose, you may find yourself questioning your own purpose, and then who will give you an answer?"

"Excuse me, but you go too far," I said. "Purpose is in the nature of the sciences, that they may increase our knowledge. As Galen advanced from Hippocrates, so we must advance from him, further toward the truth."

"And why should the truth wait for your encounter?"

By this stage the examination of the organs appeared to have reached its conclusion, and the anatomist was inserting a sharpened straw or quill into the intestines. He then brought a lighted candle to the further end of this little pipe, at which a bluish flame burned for a moment. Later my companion explained to me that the color, size and duration of the flame were all held to be matters of possible significance in the various arrangements and calculations to which the whole of the assembled observations would be subjected. After watching this instant of the flame we continued in conversation, and I fear I must have missed many other trials, samplings and measurings carried out by the anatomist and his assistants on the steadily emptying corpse.

"Truth is all around us," he continued. "It needs no hunting, only choosing and placing in intriguing arrangements. What can be known is known already: indeed, any effort should rather be in the opposite direction. Remind me to take you—"

"But why—Excuse me for interrupting," I said, "but why then should the anatomist and his apprentices be going about their labors? Why should they not rather devote themselves to lives of idle luxury or monastic contemplation?"

"You ask again for a justification in your own terms. Of course their activity is pointless: so is yours, so is mine. This is a problem only for those who seek some point."

He turned to look as the three others walked purposefully behind him toward the other table; then he returned his eyes to me. "But come," he said, "we must observe the final part of the inspection, where the anatomist attempts to read in the raveling of the brain the last thought that was in the man's head."

XXXV

in which I go with Kublai Khan
on a tour of Taidu

On that day the emperor was restless. "Come, my stranger," he said, for even after so many months he still addressed me in this way, reminding me of my foreignness but also of my closeness, for the two would have been for him associated opposites, foreigner as he was at the heart of his own empire, "we will go out and see my city."

I was astonished, for I knew the rules, how all the citizens of Taidu are commanded to stay within their shuttered houses when the imperial cortège is due to enter, pass through or leave the city, how they must lock themselves away also when the emperor goes in his robe of gold to make offerings or consult oracles at one or other of the temples at each new year or other occasion of festivity, so that he processes in splendor through the silent streets of a deserted city, like a sun wheeling through space with none to see it. I knew the popular superstition that those who deliberately or even unwittingly caught sight of the emperor's person would not require strangulation but would expire immediately in the blaze of his magnificence. It may be that I raised objections along these lines, but if so, he said: "It is precisely because none of my common people has ever seen me that I may walk among them unrecognized. There are stories that the emperor is twice the height of a normal man, that he is immensely fat, that his mustaches reach to the ground, that his body is invisible, that he has four arms, that his face shines with its own radiance, that his feet are couched in air a foot above the ground as he walks, that his raiment is transparent, that he has eyes in the palms of his hands. The people expect anything except a man such as themselves, and of course they also expect instant death should their eyes by chance fall upon the Great Khan. Seeing me as I am, they will not believe that they see me. Nor could you persuade them, not if you were to stand in the street and insist that this man beside you was the emperor, not if I were to agree that this was so. We would be taken for madmen."

And so we went out from the palace compound by the southern gate, leaving as two court officials in long silk coats and black hats, unrecognized by the guard. Nor did the cabdriver see anything unusual in his fares.

The emperor leaned forward to give him directions, which I tried to catch, for at that early time I still considered I might grow toward some understanding of the language. But of course I gained nothing from what I heard, and waited for the emperor to divulge our route.

"We are traveling toward the southwest, toward the quarter inhabited by my subjects who are followers of Mohammed. You will notice how the scent of frying pork in the air," for it was a summer evening, and we had the windows fully down, "gives way by degrees to that of boiling beef." We turned some corners, and I looked out on the little shops, the squatting children, the men in white caps or high turbans who recalled to me the stages of my journey from the further west, so that what had been an orderly succession was now jumbled and simultaneous. A child with untoward calm held forward a tray of oranges. "And this," he continued, "is Nie Jie, or you might call it 'Ox Street.' " We stopped. "You will observe the mosque, which I am reliably informed has been here for three centuries. And within its precincts you will see a tower of more recent date, which I have had them construct to assist in their scannings of the moon; for the priests of Islam are knowledgeable in astronomy, so essential a science in the establishment of a sound calendar."

"Unlike some of your court, then," I said, "you see some purpose in scientific enquiry."

"Of course," he said. "Through careful sightings of the heavens we may predict the ways of the earth. Our farmers may judge the more accurately when it is most propitious to plant rice, and, what is more on my mind, the whole empire may concur in a common marking of the days. For an unruly calendar is the sign of an unruly kingdom. That was the downfall of the Sung, that they could not call armies together from distant provinces and have them ready for battle on the same date. And that is why I am building another, greater observatory, nearer to my palace, away from the meddling imams, where I will found a school of stargazers to keep the clock of the empire in time with that of the planets. Perhaps we will visit the site later this evening" (but we did not). "Through control of time I will achieve control of space." Then he again murmured in the driver's ear, and we went on.

"We are traveling now toward the north," he said, "toward, but only a very little toward, the steppe of my past. The palace of my present is over to our right, the tomb of my future to our left." We continued through the streets of Taidu until we stopped again some way to the north of the palace, where the emperor pointed out two towers on either side of the street, answering one another like gateposts. "That on our left," he said, "we call the Bell Tower: it contains, each in its own story, four bells, ascending in diminution. The bell in the bottom story, being the largest and lowest, pitched to the note huang-chung, is struck each day at dawn. The next, again tuned to huang-chung, is rung to mark the quarters of the day: dawn, midday, dusk, midnight. And the next, which sounds at lin-chung, indicates the three watches within each quarter, while the last and smallest, again resounding at lin-chung, divides each watch into its two hours. So once a day, in honor of the eternal unity of all time, all four bells ring together, like the four seasons at once. Three times a day there are three that sound, for the triplicity of past, present and future. Eight times, for the eight ages of man, just two sound, as male and female. And twelve times, for the twelve months, a single bell is struck for the eternal unity enlaced in each hour."

I had the impression of someone repeating a lesson he had learned, speaking not for himself but for the strange empire given into his stewardship. He waited for my cue. "And the Drum Tower?" I said.

"Its construction is similar. The largest drum booms out at dawn on the first day of each new year. The second breaks with the dawn at the start of each season. The third is rapped for the first dawn of each month. And the fourth kicks at the opening dawn of each solar period: Spring Beginning, Rain Showers, Awakening Insects, Spring Equinox, Clear Brightness, Grain Rain, Summer Beginning, Full Grain, Ripe Grain, Summer Solstice, Moderate Heat, Great Heat, Autumn Beginning, Reduced Heat, White Dew, Autumn Equinox, Cold Dew, Frost Descent,

Winter Beginning, Light Snow, Heavy Snow, Winter Solstice, Moderate Cold, Severe Cold. You will note that only once in the year are all four drums beaten at once, and all four bells with them. The four drummers and the four bellmen must then feel their obligations most keenly, and all strain their eyes on the man who receives the signal by runner from the Nie Jie mosque, and drops his red silk flag from a window above us to indicate that the first hour of the first watch of the first quarter of the first day of the first solar period of the first month of the first season of the new year may begin."

At which I began to feel I was not in a city but within some elaborate chronometer, upon the face of which figures moved as the puppets of the heavens. But then the emperor asked: "Do you not see the third tower, further to the right?" I looked toward where he was pointing, and scoured the serried rooftops as if some effort on my part were needed for me to be able to see what was being shown me. "No," he said, "as yet it is only in my mind's eye." Perhaps I thought of that other tower, stopped in its building at a halfway stage but already tilting toward its destruction, as he went on: "But I cherish the notion of one day erecting another matching tower which would have four gongs within it, again rising in pitch as in placement, and dividing still larger periods of time. Perhaps the smallest could be heard at the beginning of each century, and though the following two measures are more difficult to set, I fancy the largest would crash only at the beginning and end of all time. There will, of course, be staffing problems."

Again he gave the driver instructions and we started off, passing on the right a pool. "You will have met my engineer Guo Shoujing," said the emperor, looking straight ahead from his seat beside me, so that I saw his mouth in profile opening and closing on the stream of lamplit houses that flashed by. "He is responsible for bringing water to my city from the western hills, supplying what nature failed to grant. We shall proceed against the flow of his canals, aqueducts and watercourses." So we did, and as we passed a stairway of waterfalls and debouching pipes, I was reminded of the clepsydra which the emperor had had a Chinese artificer build within its own small room in his apartments. But then soon the mounting hillbound water bore away to our right, and we entered a straight road that would lead, I reckoned, due south. Eventually the car stopped once more. "At this point I think we should get out," said the emperor, opening the door on his side and leaving me to follow him through a gateway into what I recognized as a temple. "We call this the Minzhongsi," he said. "You would say 'Temple to Mourn the Loyal.' For it owes its inception to my predecessor by six and a half centuries, the emperor Taizong, who established it as a memorial to his soldiers and generals. The pagoda over there . . ."

I lost the rest of his speech, because I was again struggling to make something out, to discover a pagoda in what was as much a building site as a palace of contemplation. Gray-robed young monks were to be seen kneeling within cool halls, and there were lay worshipers, perhaps descendants of the soldiers and generals, fanning sticks of incense before great wooden statues housed in pavilions, or prostrate in prayer on scraps of worn carpet before these same images, while only a few yards away workmen might be hammering at a wall. But there was no pagoda. Clearly the emperor saw my confusion, for he stopped— we were walking in a garden of lilies just within the entrance to the temple—and said: "I must beg your pardon, for again I refer to things I see only in my mind. The Gong Tower is yet to come; the pagoda here is for the moment past. It dates back to the Tang period, but is currently undergoing restoration."

"Restoration?" I said. "I see nothing at all."

"That is because there is nothing actually to be seen. There was an unfortunate fire here some years ago, but most of the halls have been rebuilt; only the pagoda and one or two other buildings remain. Over there you may see some of the carved pillars standing ready, and testifying to the excellence of Tang workmanship, while that hall," and he pointed to our left, "exemplifies the long, low style of the Chin of the last century: it was used by them for civil service examinations. The sleek upturned corners of the roof are very characteristic of the Chin: the Sung building to the right has, I think you will agree, an altogether stouter elegance."

"But these are all reproductions, are they not?" I said. "The original buildings were, you said, destroyed by fire."

"Their materials, yes. In some cases rebuilding has been necessary on several occasions. There was, for instance, a calamitous earthquake in the time of the Liao, whose armies had at an earlier stage laid waste the entire temple area."

"Then what we see is modern, and not really the work of the ancient dynasties of which you spoke."

"I must disagree," he said. "Of course we build with new substance, as our predecessors have done and our successors will do again, but we follow the ancient designs as faithfully as plans and memory will permit. And you will agree that the substance is immaterial. A building is not to be identified with the wood, stone and tile of which it is constructed; otherwise those heaps and stacks over there really would be a pagoda. No, a building is a figment which wood and stone and tile embody, and which different wood and stone and tile may embody at different times."

"I would say rather that design and substance are both essential, that a building is a record of its time, and as such irreplaceable. However meticulous your artisans, what they produce is a work of the present, an imitation."

"Perhaps you are right," he said after a while, turning from a ranging gaze around the temple to look again at me. "I do not as yet feel myself sovereign among buildings. The people of my nation, you must remember, live differently: the idea of a permanence, to be read in buildings as in books, is alien to us. Ours is the eternal now of wind tearing at the yurt, tugging at the leather straps and carpet roof that might the next night be reassembled forty miles nearer your Europe."

"I have known that life myself, traveling in the other direction," I said.

"Then you will know how the wanderer's free movement is in the present, whereas the city-dweller must tread on paths long laid out, among buildings that speak to him of a past before he was, of a future when others will be in the same streets, glancing at the same façades. The city—this temple—is incarnate history."

"Or forgery," I said, smiling to cover the force of my point, though I thought it would be advisable also to aim toward some touch of flattery. "The genuinely old may be a record, but the new reproduction can teach us nothing about the past, and therefore nothing about ourselves. It would be better to rebuild in the present style, not Tang or Sung or Chin but Yüan."

"That I am doing, as you know, at my great palace to the northeast of here. It will be my chapter in the book that is Taidu. But let me answer you as my ministers would. Should I impose the taste of my age on everything that falls victim to fire or other devastation? Is it not rather the emperor's duty to refurbish his inheritance as it was? For the city is a demonstration that the past is not lost but remains, and may, where ancient supervenes, be restored, not as a fake but as a reality, for the men of the past were as we are, and our skills are as theirs were. The past may become alive in us and through our labors; and just as our bodies change in substance, shedding and replenishing, and yet we remain the same, so the city lives in change but retains its memory of itself. You are concerned because the substance is not now what it was six centuries ago. But of course it is not. Wood and stone are subject to decay, as skin and hair are. The pagoda you see, or will see, is merely an instance in a chain that links our time with that of the Tang, just as the body I see before me is an instance in a chain that links you with a Venetian child. If you reject the chain but see only the present substance, then you cut yourself from the past and apprehend the world only from you own very temporary station in time. Is that not a kind of egoism?"

We returned to the waiting taxi.

XXXVI

in which the book begins
for the last time

I think the moment is here for me to become master of my own fate. If it has not already passed. So while he sleeps I take up what I cannot but regard as his pen, as if I used a man's own organ to make free with his wife. Strange I should find it so hard to take possession of these pages, which surely belong to me if to anyone. In what I have written even so far I feel myself a caterpillar newly hatched, edging hesitantly over a leaf, waiting for the diving beak. Yet I know too that this is ridiculous. The book is mine. These are my memories.

Perhaps I am too much affected by the Master of Invisible Cities and Crossed Destinies, by his suggestion that all my travels were imaginary, that every city I describe can be felt through my pages to have the contours of Venice. No doubt there is a fragment of truth in both charges, for we cannot but measure what we see by what we imagine and what we know. Yet can you not see how my accuser so much lightens his task by choosing Kinsai as his example of my palimpsests? For how could one avoid finding and recording reflections of my native city in a great trading port edging a lake and fingered by canals, a metropolis that was the greatest in China, capital of the Sung, tottering with palaces, spindly with bridges of stone, its marketplaces tumbling with fruit onto limestone pavements and silvered with fish, its squares a parade of ladies in heavy bedeckment, followed by handmaids with feathered fans to swish from them the scent of perfumes and enchantment? What other guise would you believe for a city of nobles in waterside mansions and of masters working at all the crafts of civilization, a city of gauze and silk, a city of canopied carriages and places of assignation, a city of teahouses, and bell towers, and monasteries, and boating parties onto the shallow clear waters of the lagoon? Did I not even make the analogy explicit myself, master of my own ironies? And did I not say that my description was not original, but taken from the report which the Sung empress sent on behalf of her city to Bayan, the khan's conquering warlord, the man of the north, so that your finest account of a medieval Chinese city is one man's understanding of another's version of a queen's eulogy, itself devised to fascinate an enemy into coming to loot rather than to destroy? Did I ever say I was there? Or that I was not there? Did I not, as always, keep my options open?

And what of my other cities of China? What of Yachi, where the princes of the nation sleep suspended in gray effigy on the brick wall of a temple? What of Kara-jang, where the entire populace go out in masks and fantastical attire for the holiday of Spring Beginning? What of Vochan, where there is a school for girl orphans, who give concerts of sweet music under the direction of a red-haired priest? What of Mien, where a great temple, built to house the bones of one of the chiefest bodhisatt-vas, resounds at the major festivals with the music of choirs, trumpets, oboes and violins placed all around in galleries? What of Ho-kien-fu, where lustrous objects of glass are much prized, and those that will buy them even more so? What of Changlu, where they tell of a man who found himself each night in a different bed, in a different lady's arms, waking from his sleep-walk only for those instants of ejaculation? What of Changli, where each king at his enthronement must wed the ocean, before dispersing into it the seed of his ships? What of Tandinfu, where there are special schools to instruct the people in their legendary tales, performed in song and dance and with the accompaniment of instruments? What of Sinju Matu, where every two years men and women come from throughout the world, bearing splendid images to be judged in competition? What of Linju, where on the porch of a temple four bronze horses have for centuries been on the point of galloping into the sky? What of Piju, where a great exhibition hall of paintings remains fastened because of disputes among those who tend it? What of Siju, where visitors are willing to pay dearly to take tea on a bare windy square of gloomy colonnades?

XXXVII

in which I spend an afternoon
with a concubine

Or what of Taidu, where on the lake at the winter palace, immediately to the west of the khan's citadel, boatmen sing to their passengers, partly in order to provide the entertainment and atmosphere that are expected, but also partly for reasons of exigency, since all the ferrymen who punt their long flat barks about the water are chosen from among the blind, and must sing to warn each other of their presence, and must sing also to determine, like bats, their steering from the echoes that rebound from the hillocks, temples and porcelain pavilions on the islands and around the perimeter?

Look down. At one end of the boat a wide conical rush hat obscures the boatman, except for his charcoal-clothed back arching from it and his bare arms thrust out to the right, clutching the pole which he is on the point of tugging from the water.

Apart from me and the boatman on that punted afternoon, wearing a gown of (was it?) ultramarine wantonly embroidered with gold dragons and pink peonies, was the lady. Her right arm was relaxed over the side as she sat staring back toward the Charon of our truancy. I imagined, but could not see, the tips of her fingers touching into the lake, separating three cords of long water that played there. I was facing in the opposite direction, toward whatever might be our destination, but sitting a short way back, so that she would be there fractionally first, so that we could talk at our ease. "Do you not wonder," she said, "that the emperor should allow you to make outings with one of his ladies, when only a blind man and two children are there as chaperones?"

Look down again. The boatman is at one end of the vessel. Then just ahead of him there is the same image repeated at each side of the boat, the same image of a square of blue silk, then continuing outward from the center of the boat, a round of black hair, and a cane, and a string rippling back toward the boatman and disappearing into the gray-green as it goes.

I shook my head. "I imagine," she said, "that without thinking he classes you as one of his eunuchs. Your features invite us to see you as different, and you arrived here as a party of men, not bringing any of your women, whose presence would immediately have signaled that you couple indeed as we do. Your apartness can thus include, without question, an apartness from what is not questioned." I smiled. "I hope I do not offend," she said. "Most of our eunuchs are prisoners who were taken in battle on the frontier and there castrated. They have known full manhood. They can gladden our days and moisten our nights."

Look down again. After the rush hat and the blue-shirted boys there is a considerable length of boat, empty but for a square basket, before a long oval of ultramarine, figured with gold and pink, can be seen covering two bodies.

There were no other boats in the neighborhood, and the boys were deeply intent on their fishing, and the boatman was hearing nobody but himself, and yet she whispered like one in the confessional, or like one, to come nearer my own experience, whose voice is lowered by the intimacy of a tent. Perhaps it was the ferryman's song that stretched its canvas over us. "Three men," she said, "you seem to us alone and barren. Father, son and . . . uncle, is it not? You must forgive us for seeing a mirror of procreation only in rather more populous pantheons." I smiled again. "Do I go too far? Matters of religion strike near the heart, as near as music,"—she raised her right hand in a gesture toward the boatman, and indeed white water dripped from her finger-ends, though its splashing would have been hidden by the regular swill of the punt pole—"and as love, the languages, as one of our sages might say, of the soul, the mind and the body."

Look down again. The pole is extremely foreshortened from this angle, but there must surely be four feet of it emerging from the curled blur and scar of white at the lake surface. The back of her head can be seen, and the copper gleam on her hair. His face juts out further toward the prow, and beneath.

"The boys are behaving themselves so well," she said, and indeed they sat like philosophers. "Their chance of making a catch so near the pole is small, I fear, but they have the contentment of a willing pursuit. It belongs to children, and to saints." She sighed, and looked over her right shoulder. Her fingers had returned to the water. "Has anyone yet taken you," she said, as she turned again toward me, "to the island of Qionghuadao?" I shook my head. "Then later in the afternoon we must go." We never did. "There is a famous teahouse, and a temple of the twenty-eight constellations, and a garden of jonquils, and a hall built to honor the emperor's celebrated wine bowl"—for this was early in my visit, before I had attended any of the court festivities at which the vessel brimmed with gallons of carmine from Sinkiang or yellow-green from Szechuan—"which is two feet deep and five feet wide, carved from a single stone of black jade, and decorated with sea monsters and other creatures disporting themselves in the inky waves."

Look down again. The angle of the pole, and the angle which the trailing strings make with the boat, suggest that a turn is being engineered. The other man's features are barely apparent in the deep sepia of the bottom of the boat: his expression is almost lost in shadow. It may be that his mouth is open, his eyes rolled back.

It was perhaps earlier that she said: "The distinction between us and the empresses is in rank rather than affection. They have their courts around his, and their seasons also: the empress of the southern palace must rule for the summer, the western empress for the autumn, and so on. Our infiltrations may be more fluid. Of course, each of us is bound to yield her virginity to him soon upon arrival, but thereafter our duties are ruled by his whim. Some of us may never be called to lie with him again; others may win his vigor for a week, or a month, and then no more; others slip or are slipped into his chamber at unforeseen and unforeseeable intervals throughout many years. The empresses are the drums and bells that mark out the hours; we are the flutes and shawms and fiddles that wander here and there, some played more often than others. For myself, I have been fortunate: I have borne the emperor two sons already."

Look down again. The long oval of silk, of ultramarine and gold and pink, is held by two hands seizing it from below, one on each side toward the prow end of the shape, the fingers of each hand spread wide, so wide that, even at this distance, white streaks can be detected over the tendons.

"Do you enjoy the privileges of your eunuchhood?" she said, and rested her mouth in that wide flat smile that perhaps wanted to suggest cynicism, but that gained rather my compassion for its melancholy. It is an expression I see also in her daughter, seventeen years later, in another boat as we escort her west to become the bride of the Lord of the Levant.

Look down again. The hands clasping silk, the three heads of hair, the wet arms and the indistinct face are all that can be seen of the five human bodies in the boat.

And it was much later that she said, whispered to me in a moment as we passed in a crowded hall: "It will be all right. I have arranged everything. I will be in his chamber tonight. All will be well."

XXXVIII

in which I tell
of the fourth of five visits
to places of interest in Peking

And we were again making our way along the broad forest track, at the edges of which the wind was ruffling brown leaves into momentary whorls and convolutes above the fresh grass and first flowers. Not for many months now, perhaps even years, had I enquired of the purpose or destination of our expeditions; sometimes a whole day would pass thus in silence, while we would visit some temple or ancient monument or place of manufacture, and I would be shown, and look, and know better than to ask him any questions. Perhaps this would be such an occasion. And there surely was the place, for we turned a corner in the path and had before us the prospect of a turret of glazed yellow tiles, brilliant in the almost horizontal light of the late afternoon sun, a turret of what the small windows indicated to be three stories, topped by a low-pitched conical roof that was also tiled, but in dull red. The building stood quite alone, and I think I guessed at the time that it must be part of some larger system, perhaps of observation towers (but then what could be observed from a tower that was shorter than the nearby oaks?), because I remember the Failed Sage saying, in reply to what must, after all, have been a question from me:

"It is in a sense, but a tower which observes us, which brings us into its scrutiny."

This would have been as he walked the few yards around a half of its perimeter to reach the low wooden doorway in the further side. We entered onto a stone platform that was no more than a widened step in a stairway that corkscrewed up to the higher stories and down to I knew not what, though I had no doubt that our progress would be downward. Before we went on he lit his taper, and then closed the door behind us. He led, and I followed the shadowed head that was outlined against the aureole of faltering yellow light. I did not count the steps, but there must have been thirty or so before we reached another widened step and another door, which swung inward at his touch and allowed us to enter what I perhaps thought must be some kind of mine, while the stairway spiraled on below.

But it was not a mine, or at least was not now. Instead the door had given us access into a brightly lit tunnel which extended to right and to left as far as I could see. The floor of the tunnel, where we were standing, was flat, but the walls and ceiling were continuous in circular cross section, painted in shining white, and with great numbers of lamps and torches in suspension or attachment all along. Initially, however, my eyes were more taken with the activity on the floor, where there must have been many hundreds of people talking excitedly in groups of two or three, or else standing alone, or else hurrying in one direction or the other along this subterranean pipe. Obviously something of high purpose was going on, but I could not imagine what: the intent negotiations, the determination on the faces, and the slapping steps of the runners would probably have suggested to me some sort of contest, but of course I was unwilling to test out any hypothesis on my companion before there had been further opportunity to examine what was going on. I looked at him, and he waved his arm as if to suggest that our own course might be either to left or right. I pointed to the left.

We passed several dozen of the conversing, standing and running people, all dressed, I noted, in similar robes of the palest yellow (or was that merely the color the lamps and torches imparted?) whether they were male or female. Then we passed several dozen more before one of them, a little ahead of us, dropped something, and folded himself in shadow as he bent to pick it up, and drew my attention to the ground. It was marked out in a regular grid by yellow lines crisscrossing the flagstones, defining equal squares of about a yard on each side. The breadth of the tunnel accommodated nine squares; its length was still indiscernible, and surely to be measured in hundreds, if not thousands. And I began to notice that the groups or single standers were always stationed within squares rather than across boundaries; I began to observe, too, that not all the runners were bent on courses that would take them the whole length of the tunnel, whatever that might be, but that some of them would suddenly stop on reaching a square, or else come to a square with an occupant and impart or hear some message, or alternatively arrive where there were already two or three in position and cause one of them to run on.

As we proceeded—the only two in all that crowd who seemed to be at leisure, though my mind was racing with the fastest—I began to distinguish features in the clothing of the participants. All wore badges, of either of two kinds: hard, with the design painted on wood or perhaps on some metal, and soft, with the figure embroidered on cloth. And there were three sizes of badge—large, intermediate and small—and four shapes—square, circle, triangle and crescent—and five varieties of emblem: fish, flying bird, dragon's head, bell and sword. There were six positions at which the badge might be worn: on the hat, at the shoulder, on the chest, at the end of a sleeve, at the waist, or on the back. And there were seven possible colors; but these you will know. I calculated how many different badges differently worn I might expect to see, and was not surprised that I had not so far found two guildsmen, for such I took them to be, who matched.

But of course, it suddenly occurred to me, they were not guildsmen but players in some game, which involved them in making moves about this enormous board, carrying messages and also carrying tokens of some kind, for it was one of these, I realized, that the player ahead was now picking up. And it seemed that each of the players held something tightly, so tightly that only a square blue-green corner, or a golden knob, or a vermilion curve, or a refraction from glass could be seen exposed between thumb and forefinger, or obtruding from a palm. And those must be scorers, the ones who were seated in tiny embrasures at a height of about five feet on either side of the tunnel at long intervals, looking down on the proceedings as judges from daises, or like seated effigies guarding round-arched sepulchers, or like figures of deities squashed into shrines. Yet though some of these scorers held pens and pieces of paper, though some earnestly inspected what was going on, though some leaned out in order to view more distant areas of the game, there were others who slept, or who read from books as they waited, or who had departed, leaving their perches as vacant boxes closed by doors from whatever lay beyond.

After we had passed perhaps a dozen scorers and surely a thousand players, it seemed to me that sufficient strangeness had been encountered for it to be permissible for me to ask a question, though I was at pains to introduce the tone of enquiry as lightly and obliquely as possible, for at that time I still felt that tact might be useful, if only as a politeness. "Are we too," I said, or perhaps my words were "Are we two," "players, yet have no badges and no gaming pieces?"

"No," he said, "for there is a gulf fixed between those who play and those who observe. It perhaps seems to you that there are many players, but in fact the privilege of playing is regarded among us as rare and covetable. There are many in the city who have never played, while others are repeatedly selected and have been here for many years, playing continuously, except of course when they sleep, and give their badges and marks to their shadows."

"Their shadows?"

"Yes. Each of those you see here is in reality but half a player, for each has a shadow or substitute with whom he or she shares the honors and duties of playing."

"So the game goes on without interruption?" I said. He nodded. "Then when did it begin?"

"That," he said, "is not recorded. However, from surviving accounts of the game that have reached us from centuries past, it may be conjectured that there never really was a beginning, but that the game developed gradually, imperceptibly taking on its present nature as it drew itself away from games of a different character, so that of no moment in time may we say: before this there was no game and afterward there was. For example, there is a poem of the Tang period which seems to suggest that then there were many fewer gaming pieces, perhaps only ten thousand, and that the badges were all of the same size and material, worn always at the shoulder, and distinguished by only two different shapes, three emblems and four colors. Moreover, the gaming hall of that period would appear to have been only four squares across, two thousand squares long, and four stages deep; though I ought to add that the text is disputed, with some holding that it mentions five colors and four positions of the badge, or that the hall was only two hundred squares long, or that the poem refers to some other game, or that it is a satirical allegory. Still more multiplex, though, are the arguments over a stele from the Shang periods, which some maintain records a version of the game in which there only twenty gaming pieces, disposed on a grid of two squares by twenty that was scratched on the ground."

While he was speaking we had passed on our right an exit from the tunnel, a rectangular opening a little taller than a man, and I had seen a runner almost at the top of the stairs coming up from below. Since the word "stages" had just been pronounced, I guessed that this runner must be arriving from a similar hall, and I asked how many such tunnels were stacked beneath us. "I am not sure," he said. "Possibly thirteen or fourteen." And when I asked how long each tunnel was, for still no end was in sight, he was again imprecise, saying: "There may be three thousand squares from one end to the other, or eight thousand. Few have troubled to count them, and their reports differ widely."

"But can you not consult the orginal plans?"

"Yes, indeed. However, construction work is always in progress. Even while someone walks from one end of a tunnel to the other, the end at which he started may have been surpassed, and more squares opened into the void earth, so that his tally will be inaccurate as soon as it is made. Similarly with the stages. It is hard to keep pace. When I was as young as you are, and could countenance so many stairways down and up without qualm, there were twelve levels of gaming chambers with a thirteenth under construction. Some have told me that this has long been completed and two more levels added, but others insist that the fifteenth stage is not yet in use, and it is hard to know whom one should trust."

"But why are such extensions necessary?" I asked.

"It is because the game grows, which accounts also for its continuity. The games with which you may be more familiar, and which we have also, produce outcomes: a winner, a loser, a number of points, an event of ending, a sum of money. But the game being played here, or perhaps one should rather say playing itself here, produces rules which alter its own further course. Generally, the world being as it is, new rules complicate the procedures of the game, requiring new pieces, new squares, new differentiations of the players, new levels of playing. We have records, nevertheless, of times when a new rule has greatly simplified the mechanism of the game, so that suddenly a large number of pieces will have been set aside, areas roped off, tunnels and stairways sealed, perhaps for decades. There are stories of a time three centuries ago when the game quite suddenly reverted to what I mentioned as its possible condition under the Shang, and remained in that state for several years, during slow waves of consternation that another similarly drastic change in the rules might cause it to cease itself altogether. But though there may be these perturbations, these periods of withdrawal, in the long term the progress of the game is outward, toward ever greater multifariousness. Meanwhile we who do not play wait to see what its next innovation may be: a new shape or color of badge, a new variety of gaming piece, a demand for the corridors of play to be widened."

"And those who sit outside the play," I said, "in their arched observation points: is it their function to make sure the rules are observed?"

"By no means," he said. "The game takes care of that itself, being self-disciplined as well as self-generated. The overseers are gentlemen and ladies who have come rather to examine the

game, some in order to record developments in the rules and
state of play, others to interpret what passes, for there are those
who hold that the patterns of play are thoughts that may be read.
You remember our examination of the executed man's brain?"
I nodded. "Well, some of our anatomists and philosophers believe that the operation of the brain is due to the passage of
messages and tokens to and fro through its twisting ways. From
this they argue that any similar system of messages and tokens
has the nature of a brain, and thinks. The game would be an
obvious example. Some would say that it exceeds in complexity
the brains of human beings, and therefore must be presumed to
have thoughts of transcendent wonder, but they fall into three
parties according to the conclusion they draw from this: that the
game's thoughts cannot properly be deciphered by meaner intel-
ligences; that they can be read, but only in terms limited by
human understanding; or that they will one day be elucidated
in all their revelatory splendor. Others would say that the game
is as yet less complex than a human brain, but they also fall into
three parties according to the conclusion they draw from this:
that the limited thinking capacities of the game make it admissi-
ble for us to try and make use of it for mundane calculations;
that in time the game's mental capacities will grow to equal our
own; or that this can never happen because of some essential
difference, so they argue, between nature and artifice."

"And to which of these parties do you belong?" I said.

"To none. I stand aside from disputes that can never be
resolved, in this field of expertise as in anatomy. There are no
two students of the game who will agree on the means by which
the thoughts of this brain"—I noticed at this point, waking from
concentration on what my companion was saying, that we still
seemed no nearer the end of the tunnel, though there were
perhaps fewer players in this region than there had been at the
commencement of our walk—"may be read from the movements

of messages and tokens. And even if some agreement were to be reached, it would still be impossible for any assessor to adjudge more than a tiny portion of the area of play: you see how they strain." And he pointed up to one of the little balconies, where a lady in a gown of richly embroidered silk—looking jet-black in this light, though perhaps its color was ultramarine—was bending over her parapet so that her head stuck out quite inelegantly, intently gazing up in the direction we were taking. Yet I thought him somewhat opportunist to take her as representative of them all.

"She is no doubt," he went on, "one of those who maintain that a thought of the game may be gathered from the examination of some quite restricted area. Others would say on the contrary that the materials of each thought are disposed throughout the structure, and theirs is of course the more hopeless view. If correct, it would mean that to interpret the game's thoughts we would have to station overseers to make simultaneous inspections throughout the galleries, and then have teams of runners reporting the tidings to some central point of collation, where allowance would have to be made for the different times it would have taken for different runners to arrive from different points and different levels. We should have, in effect, a second game fastened upon the first, and this too would have thoughts requiring to be read."

"Does the game have a name?" I asked.

"It is called 'K'uei,' or you would say 'The Estranged.' "

"And who is it?"

"You save the most important question until last," he said, as we came to an opening on our left, giving access to a staircase leading up. "Again, there are three schools of belief. You will hear some say that the game did not smoothly emerge but was invented, that this inventor was an emperor of the Chia dynasty, and that the game perpetuates his mind." We reached what I imagined must be ground level again, and yes indeed, my companion opened the door onto the lime green of spring grass in late sunshine. "Others say that the game is the mind of the empire, and that here are determined the appointments of ministers, the levies from provinces, the positioning of armies, the waging of war." We stepped out, and I looked around to see a turret exactly like the one through which we had entered: it might have been the same one, except that surely we must have walked a mile underground. "And there are others who adhere to the view that the game is the mind of God."

XXXIX

in which we switch on the television

It had been left by the alligator, as usual with no explanation or greeting to us but his grimace: first the stool, then the box trailing its cable to the door, clanking shut. I or he pressed the switch. A brush of electronic noised across our cell, a starburst on the screen, and then:

"Do you come out from your church feeling unsatisfied. Do you regularly feel you're not getting the service you're praying for? Have you ever thought it might all be the fault of your hosts?" We sat dumb as this image of a head and shoulders berated us. "Make sure your church isn't being left behind. Insist on HoLo Hosts, wholewheat, low salt. HoLo Hosts bring healthy eating into the sanctuary. Only HoLo Hosts give you all the goodness of God's grain *and* reduced salt. HoLo Hosts:

whole wheat, low salt. HoLo Hosts minimize the dangers of heart disease, arteriosclerosis, stomach cancer and miscarriage. Remember: HoLo Hosts, whole wheat, low salt, no additives, no goodness removed. HoLo Hosts: nothing else gives you *all* the body of Christ."

And then the padding finger and the light-brown disk were gone, to be replaced by a stained-glass window rippled by rising smoke, and a new, more relaxed voice: "We all know about passive smoking these days, but have you ever stopped to consider how much incense tar you can consume during an hour in church? It could be the equivalent of as much as five cigarettes. That's why—"

One of us reached for the knob, but the fingers stayed touched at it through a telephone call and a dream.

XL

in which he hears of his return

I said I'd go, but he was expecting a call, and so I heard only the insistent ring, his equally regular steps, the clunk as he picked up the receiver, and: "Hello . . . I'm sorry? . . . Er . . . Oh, yes . . . Yes, I'd heard from your mother, who— . . . She hadn't— . . . She hadn't . . . Oh, I'm fine . . . You're certainly sounding better . . . I mean, better than . . . You've lost . . . You're more . . . You're more . . . It's that . . . I suppose you . . . You . . . You don't . . . I imagine . . . You . . . But Bobbie said . . . Yes, she— . . . She— . . . I'm sure . . . pleased? . . . I'm sure . . . She must have . . . been pleased . . . It must have— . . . She knew it was— . . . Really? . . . more . . . But she . . . she was— . . . she— . . . It must have been— . . . I'm sure. But—goodness, is that the time? I really must— . . . We must . . . Yes, only . . . It's . . . with the— . . . But we— . . . Let's say I'll give you a call . . . soon . . . So take care . . . Ciao!"

XLI

in which I have a dream

I have a dream. The world is a boundless gray plain like a piazza
covered in fresh snow and seen in the dull light of just before
sunrise, except that there are no arcades, bell towers, churches
or mausolea to limit the blankness, which extends into infinity,
at least when viewed from one point in space twenty feet above
(no shift of this viewpoint is possible to see what is the case
behind the observer, where it might be that the world continues
identically, or ends), and yet this infinite, if we may call it so,
flatness has the air of being contained, as under some vast dome,
or underground. That would be the effect of the dim illumination, and the windlessness.

But though endless, the gray is not unbroken, for there are
many circular holes, such as eskimos might make to fish through
the ice, each being about four feet across. There is no pattern

to the arrangement of the holes, at least within the range of view. But they are close packed, so that they leave a looping network of curved triangles, quadrilaterals and struts where, in the first instant, only perfect extension of grayness has been seen.

At some of the holes, by no means all of them, perhaps two in ten, are old men who stand and, like those eskimos, fish. They are all alike, gray-bearded, dressed in mushroom-colored raincoats and brown hats, leaning forward perilously far, one would think, over their holes, each with a stick to the end of which is fastened a can, open end upward, and a line with a hook. They do not move. If the holes may be imagined as clock faces, they stand at different hours, but all unshifting, identical, motionless. Whether these immobilities are a matter of law or custom is not known. But though no movement at all is seen, though this might be a photograph, the following is believed.

The cans contain messages, written on pieces of paper. When one of the standers is successful (but would he view it as a success?) in hooking a message, he reels in his line (this part seems unlikely) and detaches the paper, then without reading it places it in his can and resumes his position as before. The theory depends, of course, on there being at least one more similar surface below this one, and yes, through the holes can be seen, about fifty feet beneath, another world of grayness, holes and bending fishermen. The eye does not reach further.

Extrapolations begin to be made. There must be some standers in the upper world whose holes do not give access to a can held out by one in the lower world. Indeed, geometry would suggest that they are vastly in the majority. Equally, there must be many in the lower world who hold out cans that none in the upper world can reach, so that their messages (but would they view them as *their* messages?) can never ascend. Is this a cause of sadness to those in either condition? Or of relief? Or of concurrence in the nature of the universe? The fixed viewpoint makes it impossible to see if there is another world above, but of course there must be, the air being filled as it is with dangling hooked threads.

XLII

in which we are still
watching the television

And the fingers broke one circuit and made another, allowing us
to hear the fading bars of something for brass quintet, and see
a design of looping triangles before both gave way to a man
saying:

"The world is full of strange, remote and isolated peoples, but
perhaps none more strange, more remote or more isolated than
the people of Yi." Imperceptibly we have been conducted to see
them, or at least a few of them, despite their strangeness, remote-
ness and isolation, dragging in a canoe from the silent waves
onto an appropriately palm-fringed beach. "The name of their
island means 'paradise,' and it would be easy to agree that this
is where they live. But it was not just to find paradise that Dr.
Giambattista Ramusio came here: what attracted him was the

language. For the people of Yi speak a lovely and lilting tongue, as calm and liquid as the ocean around them, but of particular fascination to Dr. Ramusio for just one reason: it has no word for 'I.' " The brass quintet returns, covering a cut to the straggle-bearded Dr. Ramusio, as one is to presume, seated at a table on his veranda to write in a notebook. "Dr. Ramusio first came to the island seven years ago, following reports that the language had this unique feature.

" 'Wherever you look,' " says Dr. Ramusio, though we have to guess the voice is his, since the figure at the table remains with his mouth closed, " 'you find *I*'s. In French *je*, in German *ich*, in Italian *io*, in Russian *ya*, but in Yi not anything. It is very curious, and you wonder how possibly these people can exist without such a simple and, to us, obvious word. How can they think? How can they communicate? In fact they seem to do so without difficulty.' " And we have come to see half a dozen of them sitting over a crackling fire in a forest clearing, communicating merrily, and presumably thinking with the same ease.

" 'The concept of an I,' " Dr. Ramusio was saying, " 'is a separation between inner and outer realities, but for the people of Yi such a separation simply does not exist. Of course, it is hard for us to be sure exactly what their vision of the world is, when their language is so alien, but from my own researches it would seem' "—the camera has lost interest and is scanning a group of naked children playing a game which involves rolling a green stone, while a woman nearby pounds something in a wooden mortar, and we hear the bright chatter and the regular thumps, these slightly out of synchrony with the movements of her arms, beneath the continuing voice—" 'that their thinking is completely different in those two areas where we are aware of ourselves: the area of present sensation, and the area of memory.

" 'As far as the first is concerned, the people of Yi appear not to place their sensations in themselves. If someone feels hungry, for instance, he might say *ikban doulh,* or "there is hunger," just as he might say *ikban pesen,* or "there is a house." The word *ikban* simply affirms the existence of something, without expressing it as belonging to the speaker. Indeed, in saying *ikban doulh* the speaker might actually point at someone else's stomach.' " But sadly the villagers will not be persuaded to give us a demonstration of this piquant behavior. Instead we now see five men, one of them Dr. Ramusio, remarkable for his more formal attire, standing outside a large circular hut woven from branches and grasses. Dr. Ramusio has his back to us, and would seem to be taking a photograph of the other four. And how could they register any infringement of their persons? They are perhaps even turning toward him to smile, but suddenly the vignette is lost, and we seem to be staring into gray smoke, though happily the continuing voice is unaffected.

" 'The question of memory is even more mysterious. I must confess that when I first heard about the people of Yi, I was convinced the reports must be in error, for memory would give any person a sense of his own identity, and therefore the needs for a word to signify that identity.' " We have cut to a boating party. Five splashes of water are held in miraculous stillness as gray blurs while the camera jolts with the waves and shows us a file of smiling oarsmen. " 'However, it would seem, though this I am still not sure of, that memory for these happy people is as sensation, belonging to the outer world. Their memory is only for what they can see every day: the village, their cooking pots, their fellows. Anything else has nowhere to reside in their heads. For example, I have shown them a blue enameled penknife, which caused great interest. Then I put it away in my pocket and brought it out the next day: again great interest, quite as much as before. And the next day, when I showed it to them again, their curiosity was no less. Only after a month did the penknife no longer strike them as novel: it had become a thing of the village. And it went similarly with myself. When I first arrived on Yi, I was greeted and welcomed as a stranger each morning for three months before my presence had become accommodated.' " A man stands with spear at the ready.

" 'This memory only for the unchanging has two disadvantages.' " The harpoon disappears; the man is suddenly in a squatting position drawing it up; and at the end is a twenty-pound slab of cadmium draggled with scarlet, slowly flapping its tail and adding another three to the constellation of fog spots in the way of our vision. " 'In the first place, the people are wholly unequipped for any other environment than where they grew up. But in fact they never leave. There are stories that some were seized in the last century as slaves, but when they were taken aboard a foreign vessel they became instantly catatonic, and remained so at their destination. Their reputation soon gained their island immunity from the traders. Similarly, it has proved quite impossible to teach them any other language. My own efforts to persuade them that other words are possible for "tree" or "pig" or "sea" have been met with happily amused faces and total incomprehension.' " But those faces look rather serious as the boat is rowed back to shore.

" 'The second problem is that what is transitory, like the weather or the phase of the moon, might cause each day a fearsome surprise. However, this is not so, because an old woman of the village is charged with the keeping of a calendar.' " We see her, on her haunches, under a thatched roof held up on poles, and though it is not easy to make much out in the heavy sepia shadow, she appears to be looking at rows of small objects placed on the ground, perhaps within the squares of some grid. " 'Each morning she will inform the people about the weather, the moon, the circling of the constellations, the times when the children of the village must be deemed adult.' "

. We have returned to the ball game. " 'When that time comes, she directs the pairings of husbands and wives according to ancestry. There appear to be canons of personal beauty on Yi, but of course nobody can feel a particular attraction to another person, since there is nothing to be attracted.' " It is now evening, and the whole village would seem to be gathered around the fire, cooking the fish against the crepitations of burning wood and crickets, with yellow reflections gleaming on each face. " 'A man will refer to every other islander as *pan*, which means "near" or "kin," and to his wife as *panak*, or "nearest." Their children will also be *panak* until the age of five, when they leave their parents to live in the children's house, and remain there until adulthood. Then they will be formed into couples and established in houses of their own.' "

The camera is struggling uphill through undergrowth; thick green leaves flick past on either side. " 'Until they die, when their bodies will be carried up to the mountaintop at the center of the island and there left for the crows, vultures and foxes. The people of Yi have of course no concept of an afterlife: what could they expect to go on living? And similarly there is no word in their language or action in their customs that we could associate with a sense of the divine.' "

And the fingers returned, to the off switch.

XLIII

in which I return
to the point of return

You ask why, after so many years, we ever came back. Perhaps
we never did. I sit here as my own biographer, but not my own,
rather the biographer of some other self who lived in China and
was content. The subject lends itself to self-pity, for which you
must forgive me. It is foolish to regret the past, but perhaps not
so foolish to regret the present: what dismays me is this living
in an afterglow, where everything that people want to know
about me, everything that I want to know about myself, happened half a world away. How should I not envy that other self?
And yet I wonder if his condition was so enviable. Poor wretch,
he did not know that all his impressions and encounters were
being attended by unnumbered readers, or that his journeys
were inciting so many other travels, in so many other regions of

the world and of the mind. He thought, perhaps, that he was merely living.

So what I envy is not he as he was, but he as he has become. I envy the memory of him; I envy this creature of my memory his easy access to so much that I, while creating him, failed sufficiently to recognize, to enjoy, to cherish. He may return many times—has already returned many, many times, and may do so again, illimitedly—to the island temples and the slack-watered palaces of Kinsai, to the company of a guide who will go on patiently revealing wonders to him, to the court of an emperor beginning to sense that he will never secure a hold of his mental as of his physical domains, to the park of Beihai and the arms of a concubine. I want to share that freedom of what I remember; I want to become like him a personage of memory. Perhaps that is why I agreed to this book, so that I might find space in other minds in which to roam. Was that a vain intention? We shall see, you and I; we shall see.

And now I see myself, or rather I see him, standing on the companionway of the ship, leaving the soil of China for the journey to Persia and the west. We stand, the two of us in that one body clothed in a gray padded-silk cloak, and look up to the princess standing on the deck, then back to the other lady on the quayside. We are as a mirror, for the two women, daughter and mother, have the same black hair lifted by the wind into a billowing cloud of fine scorings over what lies behind, the same intentness in their eyes, the same perfectly horizontal smile, in which might be read sorrow at a parting, courage for a venture, will for a return. We look from one to the other, from the other to the first. And I go forward to the boat while he returns to the land.

But if I could rejoin him, become an actor in the theater of memory, would I therefore lose my self-awareness? Would I become a different self? Let me hold him in my head. Let me catch him for a moment, as he steps with his companion into a yellow-tiled turret discovered in a woodland. He is aware of gloom; he wonders where he is being led; he does not know, as I know, what lies at the bottom of those steps. He does not know, as I know, that he exists only as a memory. He does not know, as I know, the truth of what he has become. And so if I am able to return, I shall not know of it. But you will. That must be some consolation.

And I return to the figure in the gray cloak, and see him from a position that was not mine, was not anybody's, see him from over the water midway between the prow and the quayside, see him standing on the plank over the glugging green and shadowy-reflective canal that separates shore from ship, see him looking now leftward to China, now rightward to the vessel, to the sea, to the east, and so circuitously to the west. And I return to his viewpoint and see now three figures at the harbor: an emperor and another old man stand behind the lady. And turning we see that there are similarly two graybeards behind the princess: my father and my uncle. We look from one group to the other, from the other to the first. And I go forward to the boat while he returns to the land.

My father and my uncle: I fear I have unduly neglected them in this account, perhaps replacing them by those two others who were their reflections at the moment of departure. Perhaps I might see us, the figment of myself and the figment of them, sitting at the end of supper one summer evening in the house that the emperor had placed at our disposal, considering whether we should leave, and how soon. We all enjoyed positions of trust, favor and responsibility at the emperor's court: he might forbid us from going. Besides which, we had grown used to a life of honor and formality. Besides which again, we had all (I can speak for them in this now that they are dead) gained entanglements of one kind or another.

So why did we leave? I remember my father voicing a wish to be buried in his native country; I remember my uncle saying how he missed his wife and children. But these were perhaps excuses we offered to the emperor, not urgent reasons in our minds. I remember my father promising we would take letters to our own emperor, concerning matters of treaty and tribute; I remember my uncle swearing we would return again, with the friars, books and blessings we had failed to deliver. But these were assurances that I have no doubt the emperor himself did not believe. I remember my father moaning in his sleep the name of his native city; I remember my uncle calling us to consider the status of the Nestorian mass, or whether confessions could be valid which were spoken in a language the priest did not understand. But I do not think we came back to find peace of mind or ease of soul. We came back because we had to. For you do not suppose we were really the first Europeans to go so far: no, many had come and lingered, some dead before we arrived, others living out their lives in palace or workshop or temple. Our distinction was that we were the first to return. We were the ones who agreed to leave our dream and enter your memory.

XLIV

in which I return to the lady
and to the princess our daughter

But I cannot.

XLV

in which I return to the theologian

Of course it was she who introduced me to Mar Sargis, builder of churches. He was an infrequent visitor to the capital, for he spent most of his time touring the country in search of lamaseries whose geometry made them suitable for refoundation as Nestorian houses: often a little paint was all that was needed, and some bread, the precious Malk of their faith, and new robes for the novices. Perhaps because I saw him rarely, I find myself unable to say much of his appearance, for in some of my memories he is a lank figure walking beside me in a cloister, while in others he is a bubble of a man waving his arms from a semireclining position on a couch, and in others he is a small, frail priest to whom I must stoop in accepting the sacrament.

We will stay with the first. "The argument is not just between us, you know," he says, though we are indeed alone as our steps perambulate again that square of ferns and old masonry. "Has your inquisiting mind never been led toward other doorways, perhaps toward our diametric opponents the Monophysites, who hold that Christ's nature is single, at once human and divine, though how they cannot say? Or toward the Apollinarians, who see in Christ a human being in whom the spirit was replaced by the Word? Or toward the Eutychians, who say that Christ's two natures were united in his baptism? Or toward one or other of the many offspring of Arius: the Exoucontians, who say that the Son was created by the Father out of unbeing; the Homoeans, for whom the Son is merely like the Father; the Adoptionists, who would have it that he was a man selected to be God, as if it might have been you, or I? Or toward the Sabellians—I rather like this one—who maintain that the Father, Son and Holy Ghost are three masks of God; and who is to say there are not more than three? Or towards the Docetists, whose view is that Christ's humanity was merely a phantasm, that he really was wholly God and not man at all? Or toward the Julianists, who conclude from this that his death was unreal? Or toward other extreme Docetists, those for whom not only Christ but all men and women, and children too, are really divine, so that if I touch you," and he stopped, and I stopped, and he placed a finger end lightly on my left cheek, and I see his blurred hand and his wide eyes as he does so, and hear his voice, "I truly touch the substance of God?" We strode on.

"But how is one to decide," I said, "among so many rival doctrines?"

"Decide? You ask this as if you might somehow make a choice, as if your choice were important. Is that not a kind of egoism?"

"But must I not choose correctly for the salvation of my soul?"

"Your choice has been made," he said, "by the nature of that soul. For surely the competing christologies are concerned not with the definition of God but of man, and of the nation. Our own faith took root not, as we might like to think, because our early patriarchs divined the truth that Christ is indeed two persons in one body, but because Persia was ready to separate itself from Byzantium, and needed a creed of its own. How else do you explain this fifth-century babble of heresies and councils if not as the noise of disintegration in the Roman imperium?" We continued our patroling of this arcaded square, our heads down, our words addressed to the cobbles.

"There was also, of course," he went on, "the inevitable extrapolation from what Christ had proposed concerning the nature of man. I sometimes like to think that before his teaching there was but one person in the world, who if he were emperor would be Tiberius, or if she were a harlot on the streets of Caesarea would take on that role: one person in a myriad of bodies. It was Christ himself," but now I think I hear him from the pulpit of his church in Kinsai, "who asked us to see ourselves as individuals. It was Christ himself who had us discover within ourselves the eternal and the temporal, the all and the ego, so that the Incarnation is a miracle happening within each of us. The danger, of course, is that in searching ourselves we shall find only a personal truth, a personal Christ. Yours," but now in this direct address he reveals himself as speaking to me alone, as we were rowed together in a barge near Suchow, "has two natures within one person, conjoined in an integrity: you therefore value integrity in yourselves, and seek to prove integrity by uniqueness, so that the words of your mouth are most importantly your words, uttered by some unified you. Whereas my Christ admits an internal division, so that I see within me many different selves, and in my body merely the housing for them all, just as Christendom houses so many Christs, even contradictory Christs: yours of singleness, mine of multivalence, the Docetists' of illusion, the Sabellians' of masquerade. There will of course," and he looks down at his finger trailing in the water, "be a time when even these possibilities will seem too few, another time of dissolution when a thousand Christs will rise in human hearts, or a thousand thousand. You have seen these temples of our Buddhist friends, with so many identical images? Except that these will not be identical. Christ's message of individual redemption will have become so much heeded that each will be his own Christ, and in that infinity Christ will disappear, as invisible as water in the ocean."

And I think it was probably at some other time that I asked him how then we might speak truth in these matters, and he said that we could do so only by repeating exactly something that had already been said, because repetition at least cannot lie.

XLVI

in which I quote
(as far as the law allows)
from the San Francisco Pacific Bell
Yellow Pages, September 1986

Assyrian Church of the East. 555 9754
Glad Tidings Temple. Sunday School 9.30 AM, Worship
    10:45 AM, Wednesday: Together we Study 7:00 PM,
    Youth Huddle 7:00 PM Parking, Nursery Care. 555 1111
Bethel Temple. 555 1433 *Please See Advertisement This Page*
Second Union Baptist Church. Radio 1450 KEST Sun
    8:30–9 PM 555 2708
Third Baptist Church. Established 1852. Dial A Prayer Call
    555 2038
First Baptist Church. Exalting Christ Since 1849. 555 3382.
    Pre-School thru 6th Grade 555 1691
Calvary Baptist Church "Soul Winning Lighthouse of San
    Francisco", 5655 Mission St (Approx. ½ Mile South of
    Geneva). 555 9190

Chinese Grace Baptist Church. 555 9090

Christ Bearers Bible Church. Friday 7:30 PM Study and Discussion of America's Historic Government, Education, and Economics. 555 5921

Buddha's Universal Church. Lecture every 2^d & 4th Sun. Chinese 1:30 PM—English follows. 555 6116

St Paul Of The Shipwreck Church. 555 3434

Mission Dolores Basilica. Old Mission Open Daily. Closed Thanksgiving & Christmas. 555 8203

Old St Mary's Church. Validated Parking Across The Street. 555 4388

Vineyard Christian Fellowship. Experience The Reality of God's Presence In Worship, Teaching, Fellowship and Healing Prayer. Call For Time & Location Of Services. 555 8700

His Way. A Christian Outreach And Service Organisation. 555 7555

Home of Christ. 555 2099

Check for expiration date on any prescription drug container. Dispose of outdated drugs. Many lose their potency and may become toxic.

Christian Life Fellowship. A Charismatic Worshiping Church Grounded in God's Word. 555 7900

The best way to make sure that buyers know what you do, is to advertize in the 'Yellow Pages'.

Miraloma Community Church. Bible Centred Faith, Christ Centred Preaching, Spirit Filled Living, Warm and Loving Congregation, Serviced by No. 36 Miraloma Bus. 555 0360

The Teaching Of The Inner Christ. Counseling, Classes, Services, Contact With Our Inner God Self. Sun Celebration & Spiritual Healing. 555 0242

First Evangelical Covenant Church. Complete Children's Program. Community Wide Home Bible Studies. 555 8755

St Gregory's Episcopal Church. Come sing God's glory. Warm, Open Community of Families & Singles, Worship with Deep Early Church Roots, Enlightened Preaching—Excellent Church School, Services in Meditation, Scripture & Personal Growth, When We Sing We Feel God's Pleasure! Look for our Banner at Gough & Bush. 555 2995

St Peter's Episcopal Church. "We Are Seeking To Integrate Intellectual Honesty & Spiritual Depth With Genuine Warmth & Committed Involvement" John B. Butcher—Pastor. 555 4942

True Sunshine Chinese Episcopal Church. 555 2160

Ecclesia Gnostica Mysteriorum. Heirs To The Mary Magdalen Line Of Apostolic Succession. 555 7412

Holy Word Church Of Evangelise China In San Francisco. 555 2438

First United Lutheran Church. Musical, Spiritual, Thoughtful & Supportive. 555 8108

Church Of New World Religion Inc. Seek Christ's "Etheric" 2^d Coming. A New Age "Christian" Priesthood. 555 8790

Church Of Christ in Pacific Heights. God's Last Mission Of Salvation. 555 3116. If no answer call 555 4750

One Mind Temple Evolutionary Transitional Church Of Christ. 555 4054

Free Evangelic Church Full Gospel. God Is A Good God. Expect A Miracle. 555 3788

Four Steps to Save a Knocked Out Tooth: 1. Rinse tooth in cool water. Do not scrub tooth. 2. If Possible, replace tooth in socket and hold it in place. 3. If this cannot be done, put the tooth under the tongue, or wrap it in a wet cloth, or drop it in a glass of milk. 4. See a dentist immediately.

Temple of Set. Intelligent And Ethical Initiation Into The Arts And Sciences Of The Prince Of Darkness. 555 9155

Metaphysical Christian Spiritualist Church And Group.
Reverend Jean Cook, G. W. Dipl., N.F.S.H. (Gt. Britain),
Principal Minister And Founder. Trance Lecture, Billets,
Healing, Meditation. 555 2295
Temple United Methodist Church. A Loving Community in
the City. Nursery thru Adult Programs. Sign Language
Interpreter. Wheelchair Access. Worship With Us. 555
1444

XLVII

in which I entertain various alternatives

There might be the story that I never left Venice, was left behind on this journey as I had been on the last, or that there was no second journey, or that there never had been a first. I might have told him stories I had remembered from nights before a log fire in our long gallery, watching the red light shine on my father's hands, sturdy between his widespread knees, as he indicated the height of a tower, or the weight of a block of jade, or the sway of an argument. Or else these might have been tales that anyone could have picked up on the Rialto, blown on the wind above the noise of bawds, bells and money-changers.

Or there might be the story that our journey took us only as far as Cyprus, or Acre, or Ayas, that we stayed the whole time there, in that hesitant eastness, in the drifting presence of houris, and returned only from boredom, or because of some scandal, or for want of money. We might have heard sufficient of the further Orient from other travelers. We might have had liberty enough to dream up our own descriptions and anecdotes. Or we might have been taken by surprise when we returned and were asked to account for ourselves, so that we spilled out our tales in spontaneous improvisation, and then in repeating them found them to be gaining the firmness of truth.

Or there might be the story that we reached only as far as Persia, or Turkestan, or Sinkiang, before turning back. Or perhaps we might have gone further than is recorded, crossing the Pacific to Japan, to Fiji, to California, but remarking only on what we thought might be believed. Or we might have gone indeed to Peking and returned from there, but had experiences quite different from those we described, because we could describe only what is describable.

Or there might be the story that we never returned, but that he, hearing in Palestine of our existence, wrote for us an imaginary travelogue, and introduced the story of the dictation so that it might be taken as genuine, in an age when such nice distinctions seemed necessary, or at any rate possible.

Or there might be the story that even my name is a part of his fiction.

XLVIII

in which there must be
a story about a well

And we were still walking around that cloister, speaking of the one and many Christs, when he took me by the arm and led me inward, through one of the archways that bisected each side, to the center of the square, where there was a well, with a simple wooden winch, and an iron bucket hanging from a rope.

"Would you care to draw up some water?" he said, and though I could neither see nor imagine any reason for doing so, I could not see how to refuse without appearing merely churlish. Besides, I had heard that Mar Sargis's suggestions, though they might be surprising, were never, as those of others sometimes were, meaningless. So I began stiffly to turn the handle, and stiffly in jolts the bucket began to descend, banging against the sides of the well as it went, fainter as it plunged deeper, giving us the impression of a bell sounding from further and further off, as if we were riding away from some city pealing with the dawn. And then it stopped, but with no satisfying splash. The rope was fully out and tense: twisting fibers stuck out as threads of sunlight from the vibrating vertical. I looked down, and could see the bucket almost at rest, with around it an annulus of black water, probably several feet beneath it.

"The rope is too short," I said, a little breathlessly. "The bucket cannot reach the water."

"Precisely," he said, brightly satisfied, as if he had accomplished some mathematical proof. I was more than a little irritated.

"But what," I said, "does this have to do with the future?"

"Do you still not see? Simply because you cannot experience the future, that is no reason to suppose it is not there, just as the water is there even though it cannot be reached by the bucket."

"Well, of course I realize that. But until the future has become past, we cannot say what it is like."

"I would rather say that we cannot *understand* the future until we meet it. The book I mentioned contains an entry, as I said, for every day from the creation of the world until the last judgment, but at any moment the entries for future dates appear totally mystifying. For instance, there was something about a well in the sentences devoted to today, but only now, now that the event in question has happened, do I recognize that a well was meant."

"There would seem to be some scope here for self-deception," I said, and perhaps he said: "How could we avoid that in the deciphering of a text?" But I know I said, nevertheless: "I should very much like to see that book."

"That may be possible," he said, "but I think that to you the whole volume would be incomprehensible: it is of course written in the ancient Syriac language of our rite. However, you must come next Sunday, when we are having one of our ecclesiastical experiments."

I did so, I believe, and have transcribed the liturgy elsewhere in this book.

XLIX

in which we exchange stories
and responses as an alternative
to all that has gone before

Kinchai was renowned for his excellent good humor, which
extended for precisely one hour each day. During that hour
he would eat heartily with his companions, empty his cup time
after time, grasp a fellow about the shoulder with his strong
right arm and rock with merriment. Lewd stories bubbled from
his lips in streams broken only by his belches and enjoyment.
Sweat seeped from his brow and gleamed. His laughter was deep
and dark, like a beef broth, or rough and unkempt, like the bark
of the danzhu. And afterward, from the latrines, he could be
heard cheerily singing songs of springtime and licentious-
ness.

But for the remainder of each day he sat in silent contemplation, in his room, on the bare banyan boards. There was no

window, only a simple doorway, and the walls were washed over with white. Against one wall, on the master's left side, stood a gong and a beater, which he was never heard to use. Behind him, high beside the door, was a silk scroll bearing the single character Kô, brushed to perfection. It was, someone said, Kinchai's last work as a calligrapher, preserving a half second still in his room from many years before.

One day the novice Chiashen entered the room and knelt before Kinchai. After remaining silent for half an hour, he said: "How beautiful is that Kô!" At this the master bounded to his feet, snatched down the scroll and tore it across the painting. In the fibrous rip of the silk Chiashen smelt enlightenment.

As long as he did not notice the fact, and find that enlightenment, like beauty, is destroyed in the instant of its recognition.

There was a peasant living in the village of Heifo who had a wife and two small sons dependent on his toil. Fengshu, who had attained a high level of wisdom, was traveling in the area and came upon the man sowing rice. The peasant, being bent over at his work, did not see the master, but only heard the words: "Follow me." At once, without looking up, he put down his basket of seed, then stood, and went after the man who was already stepping away up the field: a stubble head, a yellow robe a sail in the breeze. Neither spoke, until after they had walked nine miles Fengshu turned to the peasant and said: "Go back to your family." The man did so.

The wise course is to follow no advice, not even this.

One day Pietro and Sandro were walking past a large and ancient juniper tree which was thronged with finches. "How many birds do you suppose there are in that tree?" Pietro said. Sandro immediately stopped and sat down a few yards from the tree.

Two days later Pietro returned. Sandro was still sitting in the same position, and hoping to forestall his master's question he shouted out: "Two thousand, four hundred and one." Pietro advanced to the young man and beat him hard on the left shoulder with his staff.

Not all answers are worth giving, especially to questions that were not worth asking.

Danshao was strolling through a field with his four disciples. "Consider the lilies," he said. "Which part of them most resembles your Buddha nature?" "The petal for its purity," said the first. Danshao smiled. "The leaf for its green of celestial peace," said the second. Danshao smiled again. "The seedhead for its fruitfulness," said the third. And again Danshao smiled. "The leg," said the fourth. Danshao's face immediately turned crimson, and sparkling droplets flew from his mouth with the sound of his rage.

The master answers the stupid civilly. How else should he answer the wise?

Two monks were seated gazing toward a distant range of hills. "The enlightened soul is not limited in its extension by the body," said the elder of them. "Can you transport your inner self to the heights of that ridge?" The younger monk did not answer; both continued staring ahead. After an hour the elder said: "Are you there yet?" "No," said his companion. Then after a further hour the elder monk repeated his question. This time there was no reply. "Is the rice sprouting in the valley beyond?" said the elder monk.

His fourth and final question must be addressed to the reader, since even this old fool must know that the soul has no eyes, no ears, no mouth.

The unenlightened mind will not have patience for so many meaningless anecdotes.

But a scrap may lure it.

"Does the spider have Buddha nature?" Kei Po once asked his disciples. "Yes," said one of them, "because she is in perfect equilibrium with her environment, because she has the capacity for long stillness and quick action, because she creates beauty unconsciously, because she is silent, because—" Kei Po took off his left sandal and threw it at the boy.

In the algebra of the soul, addition cannot but be subtraction. Kindness is a pretty dubious concept too.

Does the universe seem to you unimaginably ancient? A slug gifted in arithmetic and knowledgeable in geography once said to herself: "How wide is the world! For me, traveling without rest, two hundred thousand years would not suffice to journey around it. What a tiny part of the whole is mine!" She did not see the migrating birds, or hear the voice of the whale. Do not, therefore, mistake your perception of time for its reality. Was there passing time at all before the fine disciples of memory known as language and music? The universe may be only a few hundred generations from its birth.

Don't tell me: to the enlightened mind it starts and stops now.

Paolo, standing at his bench, dropped a glass beaker, and watched it fall away from him, like a coin through water. He saw the glint of the first crack, saw it spread, forking like yellow lightning through the material as pieces detached themselves and spun away, great motes in the sunlight. He heard a noise like the roll of a wave, far away. Far away Maria was at the theater with her new lover: afterward she was amazed that two hours had passed so quickly. Luca was asleep.

How come they didn't have arguments with the clock?

.

On his way eastward across the island, once he had reached the village, he felt at last the intimate nearness of nature, like air, infiltrating his being with the nattering burr of a bird, the whistled reiterated prayers of crickets, the whispering of bamboo. Returning westward he smiled at his foolishness: he had not once turned to see the twin towers of the power station, the torso that quarries had made of the peninsula beyond the bay.

The wise man, in his penetration of the world, is as little disturbed by what he sees as by what he does not see. But who is this ass who rejoices in the absence of people and then places them there in his words?

Che Han said: "The higher knowledge consists in imagining a color midway between green and silver. The higher wisdom consists in conceiving an animal intermediate between the tiger and the phoenix. The higher understanding consists in apprehending a whole number between one and three which is not two."

And how did he prove his achievements?

"If the passage of time is an illusion," said Gemoveva, "how is it that I cannot wake myself from it?"

Because who could willingly leave a dream?

The man was stopped at the water's edge, sifting river gravel, with at his waist a leather pouch into which his fingers slipped gobbets of gold. The monk came up from behind and stared into the man's pan, then reached in and extracted a small piece of rough gray grit. The man looked up at him as he turned it in his fingers for some minutes, smiled and said softly: "How beautiful!" But hardly had he finished these words when he felt the man's hand behind his knees and the sudden ice of the water.

The enlightened spirit should find correctness in all things, including the behavior of others.

"And then he gave away all that he had," said Niccolò, "even his clothing he returned to his father."

But not his name. The greatest saints vanish into anonymity.

"And then he gave away all that he had," said Niccolò, "even his clothing he returned to his father." The old abbot sat expressionless. "And he conversed with the birds, telling them of salvation."

He should have cast his words within, not troubled the incorruptible.

"And then he gave away all that he had," said Niccolò, "even his clothing he returned to his father." The old abbot sat expressionless. "And he conversed with the birds, telling them of salvation." The old abbot made no response. "And he bore on his body the five wounds."

The good act can never be repeated.

"And then he gave away all that he had," said Niccolò, "even his clothing he returned to his father." The old abbot sat expressionless. "And he conversed with the birds, telling them of salvation." The old abbot made no response. "And he bore on his body the five wounds." Still the old abbot sat silent and unmoving. "And finally he died." The old abbot's eyebrows jumped to his forehead and his mouth was a cave.

Excellent it is to be astonished only by the banal.

The emperor opens his casement. The air is scented with hyacinths; pink noiselessly explodes on the cherry trees; a flash of orpiment is a yellowhammer rocketing up to her nest. He says softly to himself, as if for the hundredth time: "Why is it springtime?"

Does no one hear the springtime asking: "Why is it he?"

A teacher once said to his pupils: "You are walking along a road, looking straight ahead, with to your right a continuous glade, and the sun fingered by the branches. In the distance you see a large dog running toward you, now white, now suddenly gray, and again white, gray, white as he lopes unheeding through irregularly spaced patches of sunlight. He is perhaps three hundred meters from you." The teacher was silent for precisely fifteen seconds, and then said: "Has he passed you yet?"

Doesn't he know that the mind's chronometer stops if not wound with words?

In another version of this story the teacher's silence is broken after twelve seconds by one of his pupils crying out that she felt the quick warm brush of thick fur.

Does he still wait and put his question?

In yet another version of the story there is a wait of only eleven seconds before one of the pupils tightly sucks in air and moves his left hand to his left calf. It is not recorded whether there were toothmarks.

Does the teacher apologize?

In still another version the silence is duly completed and the question put, but is immediately answered by a bark.

Does he have any right to be surprised?

One further variant has it that the silence is unending.

Matteo was sitting with his students in an orchard of plum trees, against one of which the harvesters had left a ladder having five rungs. "The ascent to God is like this," he said. "You must climb that ladder taking each step as if it were the first, forgetting any steps behind you, forgetting even the way of climbing ladders." One of the students was bold enough to make the attempt. He stood at the bottom for a minute or two, breathing deeply, then with sudden force he stepped onto the first rung. Again he stopped, and again his fellows heard the effortful wind of his breath above the papery murmur of the leaves. Then after perhaps five minutes he stepped up again, just as quickly, with bulging determination in his face. Once more he stopped, and it seemed that his lungs might burst from the pressure he was putting on them. This time the wait was longer still: it may have been a quarter of an hour before he leapt up to the third rung, and then a full hour before he reached the fourth. All this while Matteo and the other students sat watching the climber's progress, and stayed silent, listening only to his breath and the birds and the leaves, even during the three or four hours that elapsed before he made his bound to the top. But then at once Matteo spoke: "Fool!" he said. "Even the greatest masters have waited a lifetime before making the first step. None has ever taken the second."

Foolish Matteo not to be constantly expecting the unprecedented.

Some hold that the climbing student made the first rung, then waited for an hour and fell off. Matteo's response in this case is said to have been more generous.

But this Matteo is a fool too if he thinks the tremblings of the body can indicate the elevations of the soul.

Guglielmo spent thirty years in the study of a single painting which had been done a century before by one of the masters of his city: it was an Annunciation. With rulers, dividers and protractors he plotted the positions of the lady and the angel and the columned portico behind; he came up with several theories about how the panel might have been planned geometrically. He analysed the pigments, and discovered that the angel's gown probably owed its green to an outcrop of malachite in the vicinity, that the shadow of the unlit windows was almost certainly a compound of lampblack and gun tragacanth, that dried and powdered horse blood was very likely what gave the Madonna's hair its luster of copper. He researched the painter's life, and made out a convincing case that the angel and the lady (for certainly they were much alike) were both portraits of the master's mistress Giovanetta, one full face (the Mary), one showing the right side of the face in profile (the Gabriel). He also formed views, as sophisticated as they were inventive, on what other treatments of the subject the painter might have seen. And many or all of these hypotheses he would unfold with energy to anyone new to the city, seizing his victim by the shoulder and marching him or her to the church where the painting hung.

One afternoon he was there with a visitor, expatiating on the meanings woven into the monograms, fruits and flowers of the lady's belt, when he was stopped by the sound of footsteps, echoes splashing of hard leather on the ancient tile, as a young woman came into the chapel. He, but not his companion, looked round, and watched open-mouthed as the girl stepped forward, said "Lovely, isn't it?" then turned and walked away.

What isn't known instantly isn't worth knowing. What's said instantly isn't worth saying.

A poet and his son were sitting at table. The poet picked up a small silver coin and held it a foot or so above the table, then looked gravely at his son and asked him if, seeing the coin drop, he would be able to clap his hands before it landed. "Yes, of course," said the boy, and held his hands ready, fixed his eyes intently on the coin. Yet still the chink of metal on wood came before the slap of flesh on flesh, and so a dozen times before the boy smilingly accepted defeat.

Nothing ever happens.

While the coin was dropping for the first time, a green-eyed woman in a courtyard plucked a note on her lute, another woman in a Persian square had a thought, a man kicked a wooden boat, words were written in a hotel bedroom in Saint Louis, and the boy realized he was not going to make it.

Everything is always happening.

While the coin was dropping for the second time, a young man spotted another bird, a monk spoke a plosive in the middle of a question, a slug had an idea, more words were written in a hotel bedroom in Saint Louis, and the boy realized he was realizing for the second time.

Happening isn't something that anything can do more than once.

Queen Elizabeth I thought long and hard before giving her consent.

Foolish woman: she should have consulted her Buddha nature.

Thereupon the king asked the caterpillar who had made the world.

And what was his question?

There was a master who taught that nothing could be used that was not owned, and nothing could be owned that was not possessed in spirit. He might be seen seated before his house, leading his disciples in silent contemplation, each of them gazing on some object he or she had brought to the lesson: a writing brush, a jade clasp, a bronze knife for opening letters. The work of mentally accomplishing these things was obviously arduous, and sometimes the sun would go down on the hushed white-robed circle. But then the master retired to a lamasery, which would be startled at night by the lightning of his shrieks and the thunder of his feet. One morning, after the monks had been spared these alarms, one ventured into his cell and found him naked and dead, the food of three weeks untouched.

The greatest folly is to address the spiritual mind to the material world. Is that it?

Jenko, a treasured composer of songs, decided one day that he must free his music from the confines of his taste, and so he began to compose according to rigid rules, demanding of himself, for instance, that a song should consist of just one fragment of melody many times repeated, or that all the notes of the mode be used before any could reappear. His audiences found the results perplexing, but they appreciated his scrupulousness. Then he decided that his systems were themselves inventions of his own, and so he began to compose according to chance, placing notes as the falls of dice determined, or in consultation of a book or oracles. Now his audiences were still more perplexed, but their appreciation of his scrupulousness was if anything enhanced. But then he decided that his random methods were also devisings of his own, and so he began to compose, if the word may still be used, without making any definite prescription, presenting his musicians with enigmatic diagrams, or impossible instructions, or blank sheets of paper. Naturally this increased even further the perplexity of his audiences, but it increased no less their appreciation of his scrupulousness.

But then he decided that the world was something he'd imagined, and there was nothing he could do about it.

Part of the course was the study of a painting which consisted of thirteen identically sized panels, each a hundred and fifty centimeters deep and forty centimeters across, each painted all over in a different color, the thirteen abutting one another to make a broad rectangle of vertical stripes: bright primrose, apple green, leaf green, bottle green, royal blue, hyacinth, purple, claret, scarlet, tangerine, orange, yellow orange, bright mustard, reading as was customary from left to right.

The master left his student in front of the picture for ten minutes and then returned to ask her what she had seen: she gave a description rather similar to that contained in the preceding paragraph, except that she remarked how the colors formed a circular progression, since the bright mustard at the right could join in nearness with the bright primrose at the left, and so one might imagine twelve other paintings in which the circle had been broken at other points. Perhaps she also pointed out that the closeness of the colors was their closeness in the spectrum, except that the linear spectrum had been made circular by the artifice of a nonspectral junction between the red and violet ends, as if the rainbow had been curled into a tube of colored air; and she could not decide which of the central colors, the hyacinth, the purple or the claret, formed this junction.

Without making any comment on her answer the master left her again, and again returned after ten minutes. Now what she described was something much simpler: she saw adjacent pairs and triplets of panels blending briefly into an average, so that the three leftmost panels might become almost a square of lime green, or the claret and scarlet might flow together as a fat stripe of cherry red. And though she tried to forge foursomes together in her mind, this proved impossible: indeed, the meldings did not seem to be subject to conscious control. Still, she thought she knew what would happen if ever the entire thirteen were to be seen as one.

Without making any comment on her answer the master left her yet again, and yet again returned after ten minutes. Now what she described was something much more complex: between the bands of color she saw waves of intermediate color, and then human figures and landscapes and abstract designs flashed and swept across the surface before her.

"Provided they represent the full circle," he might have said, "the most rudimentary instances can convey the all." She might then have spent the rest of her life signing sheets of white paper, in a state of detachment that sometimes caused her to wonder and to regret.

Fankiu was once entertained to dinner by a Persian merchant, who shared with him first a stew of chicken, apricots, ginger and almonds, presented in a fine bowl of Nishapur. As servings were removed, Fankiu noticed that the inside of the bowl was decorated with a border of falling black ribbons and tassels which perhaps was to be understood not merely as ornament but as a text. He asked if this was so, and the merchant confirmed that it was, supplying the translation: "Planning before work protects you from regret. Prosperity and peace." The bowl was removed, and replaced by another, containing a pudding of malted grains, figs and grapes. Again Fankiu asked about the collar of black strokes and curlicues that was revealed as they ate, and again the merchant offered a translation: "Knowledge is the beautifi-

cation of the youth; and intelligence a crown of gold. Blessing."
Fankiu then rose to leave, and said how appropriate it was that
lies should be written on pottery, where they might break.
*The guest shows his obtuseness in not realizing that planning and
knowledge have their place, in the kitchen.*

Piero once took his disciples into the forest. "Do not envy the
trees their longevity," he said. "They merely live more slowly:
a year for them passes as quickly as a month for us, since all
consciousness is defined by the period of its existence. Similarly," he went on, "do not pity these butterflies," for two
beige-winged creatures were flickering around each other in the
air where he pointed, "the shortness of their lives: a single
second for them has the length of an hour."
*Under his right foot was a pebble, for whom his speech lasted a
microsecond, so that it remembered him as little as you remember
the half second. when our eyes met.*

There was a teacher called Shaotsung who had seven pupils in
whom he was trying to inculcate an understanding of music. He
played them a record, but raised the needle after the first sound
had reverberated into the studio. Then he asked his students to
write down what they had heard. The first wrote: "This was the
opening chord of Beethoven's *Eroica* Symphony." Shaotsung
clenched his teeth, pulled his lips back in a fierce grimace, and
tore the paper to shreds.
For who would pretend to hear what only all may hear?

The second student wrote: "This is a chord of E flat major being
played by an orchestra of early nineteenth-century proportions.
Though the particular work is unfamiliar to me, I would guess
the composer to be Beethoven, though Berlioz and Schumann
would also be possibilities, nor could I entirely dismiss the
conjecture that this is from an early work of Wagner's, even if

the presence of three horns in the orchestra, at least, I think there were three . . ." Shaotsung had no opportunity to make a comment on this student, since she is still writing.

For who would pretend to complete what only all may complete?

The third student wrote: "I see a young man of haughty mien, seated on a charger; he wears a long gray coat, and a cocked hat in a darker gray. And in the echoing I hear the noise of battles." Shaotsung did not understand this answer.

For the teacher has his speciality.

The fourth student wrote: "I am reminded of when I first heard this work: it was—" Shaotsung did not read any further, so great was his fury.

For the teacher has his pride.

The fifth student wrote: "I hear a pen scratching symbols on paper, racing against the impossibility of recording in an instant what has been imagined in an instant." Shaotsung rather liked this answer, but would not say so.

For the teacher is not to be presumed guiltless.

The sixth student wrote nothing. When Shaotsung asked him why, he replied: "The sound was too beautiful for words to express." Shaotsung's outburst in this case is said to have been rather alarming.

For ignorance must not be stupid.

The seventh student also wrote nothing. And when Shaotsung asked her why, she made no reply. She became his favorite pupil, though he was never entirely convinced of her worthiness.

For ignorance must always be mistrusted.

Stopped in a column of taxis in a traffic jam, Fabia turned her eyes toward a large blank wall on the left of the street, where the sun had cast up shadows of the waiting cars, their outlines vapored in its and their own heat. By observing the angle of the sun, she tried to determine which of the shadows contained the shadowy figure of herself. It troubled her that this should remain uncertain. But then the line moved on.

Who is this requiring the heavens to prove her existence?

"But we cannot be characters in a book," Marco retorted, "for think of the vast amount of detail the author would need to supply in order to create a world such as this." He gestured expansively with his right arm and cast his eyes about: I was standing beside him, on a lawn in the imperial gardens. Then he reached down and picked a blade of grass: "You see here the fine bright veins, and the shape which is this blade's alone, and the specks of dirt which also define it? Could an author invent this and also the myriad others of the lawn, let alone the remainder of our universe?"

Yet he was asking only for a blade of grass to be sketched in three phrases.

On another occasion Shaotsung took his pupils up a mountain to observe the sunrise, which he said would be more beneficial to them than hearing Beethoven's *Pastoral* Symphony. They watched the world change from black to gray to correctness, and admired the view over a small village, where, with slow thwacks that echoed in a quick duplication, a peasant was chopping wood. At least, they all watched and admired these things except for the third student, who was blind, and whose tears eventually became sobs, so that all the rest turned to ask what was distressing him. He described a town, a square, a silent crowd, a scaffold, an executioner decapitating victims as rapidly as they could be forced before him.

There remains the possibility that the seventh student was deaf.

"The self festers in the enclosure of introspection," the master once said. "Free your nouns from the adjective of your self."
He was not trying to write extended prose.

And so I wondered, while crossing Tennessee on the 18:45 Continental flight from Houston to Gatwick CO 046 on St. Patrick's Day, 1987, at what point belief in me might evaporate as I talked about my page, my handwriting, my lengthily delayed second cadence, or the sixth letter of which I am constituted. *The enlightened mind distrusts all first-person voices. Especially its own.*

There was another of these anecdotes, but I have forgotten it. *The response, however, is contained in all that follows.*

L

in which I speak with the emperor

After the sacrifice, as he was leaving in procession through the press in the outer temple, he caught my eye, and I elbowed my way to join the jostling cluster that came after the stately line of dignitaries led by him through the shuttered streets of the city back to the imperial palace. The slowly marching column and its unruly aftermath, like an exclamation mark of which the stop has been smeared, passed through the southern gate and came to the Hall of Eleven Virtues, where the emperor was to be disrobed. Most of those in the informal part of the assembly made their obeisances at this point and departed, while the functionaries went in and so to their places of work or rest. I went up onto the single wooden step before the entrance, and stood with one hand at the left doorpost, my fingers gripped into the deeply incised carving of spiraling foliage painted in red and gold.

This was one of the smallest buildings within the palace: the chamber into which I looked was perhaps no more than thirty feet square, and though only weak light came into it through the doorway, I could see the calligraphic hangings on the wall beyond, and the emperor standing in the middle of the hall, with some official on the right ceremoniously removing the coat (which I seem to remember being of an ultramarine color) that the sacrifice had required, while two servants were kneeling before him, perhaps waiting for orders, perhaps ready to take the coat, or perhaps, like heraldic supporters, fulfilling the needs of pictorial nobility and symmetry. I imagined, or perhaps I only now imagine, that somewhere there must have been a wardrobe that was a missal of rites and seasons, containing the garments that the emperor would have to wear for the new year, for his birthday, for the veneration of his father, for the day of the dragon, for the prayers of spring sowing, for the sacrifice we had just witnessed of barley grains and herbed wine tossed odorously onto a fire of black stones kept burning on the altar of the Temple of the Sky Princess. And indeed the coat was laid over the four arms of the kneeling servants, who rose and departed with it through one of the side doors that gave entrance to corridors leading to other parts of the palace. Following a nod from the emperor, I replaced them in the chamber; a second nod dismissed the official, leaving the two of us to sit side by side in chairs that faced the main doorway, so that as we talked we could see people walking to and fro in the midday light that appeared so blinding and hazy from the darkness out of which we watched.

"So did you follow the ceremony, my stranger?" he said.

I had to confess that the meaning of what I had seen was

hidden from me, for lack of knowledge of the language and customs.

"It is so for me also," he said, but in his case any regret seemed to have been stilled. "I have been ruling here for . . . what: twenty years is it now? It would depend, I suppose, on whether one is counting by the lunar or the solar calendar. Nothing in this country is single and definite; nothing is to be grasped as tangible fact. Knowledge rather leaks into one slowly, and by the time it has arrived, one has ceased to recognize it as new or unusual. Where nothing is understood, nothing can surprise, and one finds oneself wandering without hope of illumination or shock." Possibly there was then silence while people continued to pass before us, and a bee, gilded with sunlight, etched figures in the top left corner of the door opening.

"Consider this ceremony," he went on, "which I have performed now, let us agree, twenty times. There was never any question of explanation or rehearsal, of course: if I was the emperor, I must know. Fortunately, because at first my knowledge of the language was even more hesitant, there were no words to be spoken—or if there were, nobody ever remarked on the fact, or thought it strange that I said nothing: it could be, I suppose, that this was once a voluble ceremony which I have rendered into silence, as I have others. But my movements of hands and feet were shaped and guided by some of them who had served my predecessors, so that I was a doll they operated. Now, of course, there is no difficulty: I go through my motions as emperor with confidence, and even—would you not agree?— aplomb, even if my understanding is no more than it was when I was their puppet." He turned to look at me (if I remember rightly, he was on my left); I bowed my head.

"My stranger," he continued, "you are the only one to whom I can speak so, stranger here as I myself am, both of us becoming less estranged as hour succeeds hour, minute minute. You know how they distinguish two categories among us barbarians, the raw and the cooked, according to how much of their culture has been steamed into us? You are raw, as I was. But now I have spent long years in their pans and kettles. I am cooked, and perhaps dead: no longer a warrior of tent and saddle, nor yet a silk-gowned inhabitant of teahouses, belvederes, jonquil gardens and masked theaters." I imagine again there was a pause. "Perhaps it is simply that I have reached the age at which the patterns one has formed begin to dissolve and separate in the excess waters of too much experience. Or perhaps it may be your arrival that reminds me of the certainty I once knew in my difference from these people, as distinct from the uncertainty I know now that I am closer to them. For do I not now speak, read and even write their language with tolerable facility? Have I not encouraged the perpetuation of their ancient customs even while accepting new learning from elsewhere? Do I not play my part in their ceremonies without guidance, as if I had been brought up here a prince of the Sung, petted by feathered empresses, concubines and eunuchs, not suddenly imposed after a youth of martial rigor as far away as Hungary and Silesia?" I could have asked him at this point why they never conquered further. A servant arrived with two bowls of tea and a plate of crystallized cherries.

"You may well wonder why we did not go to Vienna, to Rome, to Paris, even to your Venice, to make your San Marco our stables and its square our exercising ground." He spoke, of course, amusedly of the role we Europeans had, in our fear and ignorance, given his people, though as I hear his voice again, I detect in it also a weariness, as if it might have been easier to have accepted that role. "Were we simply the enacters of your nightmare of retribution, a retribution that had to burst upon you after so long crusading into the east? Not in our action, of course, where we lived our own dream, but in your interpretation, and in the way your interpretation became a cause of events, as dreams will color days that come after. And did we then retire, perhaps, because you awoke? And does the east, I wonder, dream the west, too, as the west dreams the east? Are your geometries and purposes and mechanics and moralities the substance of our dreams, as our pinnacled pagodas and odalisques and silks and fountain-splashed courtyards are the substance of yours? Does each of us have to live half a life, leaving the other for the night, turning as the earth turns between light and darkness, life and dream? Does the choice have to be made between Buddha and Christ?" And I imagine these questions spoken softly, almost murmured, for they are no doubt questions the emperor had voiced many times, including many times in my hearing.

And at least once, though possibly not on this occasion when we sat watching a world moving in the noon brightness within and beyond that narrow rectangle, I would have spoken of the messages from the pope, of the ostensible reason why we had come. Indeed, as I recall these matters I begin to recognize that we must have considered them many times, but with results that were always negative in the same way, our discussion fanning out into a delta of questions, the movement of our arguments becoming turgid, our engagement in them desultory, so that what had been a brisk, lively and impassioned exchange, on both sides, would end on both sides in slow, dreary dejection. There were always the same silt banks of objection and unwillingness. If the emperor were to recognize Christ, would he have to dissociate himself from other ceremonials? Would he have to encourage the conversion of his people? Would he be obliged to persecute the Nestorians, among whom were members of his own family, if he himself accepted the Roman faith? And if he were to acknowledge the God of Rome, would that as a consequence bind him in vassaldom to the pope, or to the emperor of the west? Perhaps it was indeed then, as we sat facing but no longer seeing the opening into intense illumination, that he voiced his doubts.

"I see myself as the water steward of a great pool in which there are many different kinds of fish. Some of the larger ones may eat some of the smaller ones, but these replenish themselves adequately by ease in breeding, and there is an overall stability, except for the rather rare appearances of new hybrids or the equally rare extinctions. Now I am asked to introduce into my pool an enormous pike, which surely will bring catastrophe to the harmony I have nurtured. For I think you are too much the heirs of St. Paul, who wrote to the Galatians of conversion as a crisis of bewilderment, or to the Ephesians of a change from death to life. This is not the sleeping religion of our Nestorians, who admit a multiplicity within the state as within the person, and who are content to join in procession with imams, lamas and fire-worshipers. I see in the west rather a fierce certainty in a single truth, a belief that the truth may be single, an insistence that in its singleness it should rule everything in our lives, as again your saints write. It follows that if we accept your religious beliefs, we have to become as you. Is that not on your part a kind of egoism? Can a tree become a dragon, or a river a horse? You ask us even to worship in a strange language, because there are no equivalences in our tongues for your concepts: God the Father, Holy Spirit, Body of Christ. These things have to be worshiped in their unity, and since translation would compromise that unity, they have to be worshiped in a single language. What could more deeply wrench us from ourselves? And if we learn your language in order to speak your Mass, are we saving ourselves, or are we rather saving those other Latin selves whom we have created within us?"

Yet in all this I realize I have not given an adequate description of the great khan. He was about sixty years of age, yet still with strong black hair that streamed straight from the edges of his bald crown. He was a little below the average height of his people, and considerably shorter than me. He was also distinctly stout, and unable to spread wide his broad fingers, as if his hands were constrained by webbing. His eyes were famously watchful, though sometimes, if he glanced at me in conversation, their watchfulness would give the impression of a never spoken pleading, even a silent desperation.

It could have been on this occasion that he told me a story.

LI

in which the emperor

tells me a story

There was a man who was about sixty years of age, yet still with strong black hair that streamed straight from the edges of his bald crown. He was a little below the average height of his people, and considerably shorter than me. Other details of his appearance need not concern us.

One day he was out hunting with his companions, as you know that I delight to do, out on horseback plucking fowls from the air with the sagittarian skills of my birth sign. But he became separated from the rest of his party, and a violent thunderstorm overtook him. Luckily, however, just as the slanting rain began to stipple his vision, he saw in the hillside to his left a black hole, and riding in that direction found a cave in which he might shelter. While there he was entertained by a peri, so that the

shudders of the sky were echoed in his genitals, which rained
also into her vagina, and then into her mouth, and then again,
such was her skill, and his lustfulness, and the stimulus of the
thunder, into her rump. As soon as he had made this last
ejaculation she vanished, and the storm ended, and he turned
to look out through the cave entrance, and saw only sunlit
brilliance such as we see now. He stepped out from the cave, and
there was no dampness on the ground, no dripping from the
trees, though his mare remained tethered exactly as he had left
her. As you might expect, he was somewhat puzzled, though
because the horse was there, and because we will overlook any
strangeness in the universe provided our immediate needs are
met, he mounted and returned to the palace where he lived, for
have I not mentioned that he was a great lord of his country?

When he arrived at his palace he gave his horse to be taken
care of and strode in to greet his wife, if with limited effusive-
ness. But while walking along a lower gallery he caught sight of
his face in a polished silver mirror, and stopped in astonishment.
His hair was much thinner, curling in its weakness and laced
with many strands of white. His face was deeply lined, and there
was a yellow-brown spot above his left eye that had not been
there before. He seemed to himself (though these things are hard
to judge) at least ten years older than he had been at the beginning of the day. So it was with understandable agitation that he
went on, calling loudly for his wife, whose name echoed four
times through the palace before he stopped again on hearing
behind him, at the distant end where he had entered, a footstep
answering his own of two minutes before. He turned and saw his
grandson, saw frenzy shaped on the flange of the boy's lower lip
(for his eyesight still was acute despite all the curious troubles
of the day), saw the lad stooped in a crouch, holding ready in
his left hand a lance. And no sooner had he registered these four
items—the grandson, the lip, the crouch, the lance—than with

a whipping sound the weapon left the boy's hand and began its journey through the prism of air contained in the gallery.

The suddenly aged lord moved to sidestep the spear's inevitable trajectory, for he surely had more freedom than it had, and surely had time enough to avoid their encounter; but he found he had no use of his limbs. The lance approached. He struggled to free himself from his point on its path, but was caught as securely as an aphid in a spider's web. While working to shift his right leg, he thought how stupid the boy had been to choose a method of assassination that would surely fail, and that in its sure failure would surely entail the would-be murderer's execution, by means which at the moment there was not the leisure to devise, though the moment for that devising would come. But the spear was still approaching, and perhaps because adrenaline is such an effective disrupter of chronometry, the lord saw it wobbling in its journey, preserving the fury of the thrust, coming toward him now silver in the light from a window, now dark gray in the shadow between. And he wondered what reason the boy should have found to choose this moment; he wondered too whether the attempted murder had been long relished, or whether it was a sudden lunge of impulse, made because he had thwarted some desire of the boy's.

Still he could not move. Still the weapon approached. And his thoughts began to become more metaphysical. But then, when the lance was perhaps only ten yards from him, directed by a certain aim, and surely due to strike him in a quarter of a second (yet what was a quarter of a second to his stretched sense of time?), it stopped, in rigid suspension, wobbling no longer. It seemed to the lord that it stayed in the air for many seconds (yet how was he to judge?), and he made to stride forward and, Parsifal-like, seize it. But still he was unable to stir his legs. And still the spear remained. Until, to his amazement, it began to glide back along its path. Then, when it had returned, silver,

gray and silver again, to about midway along the gallery, it
began without pause to come again toward him, then switched
direction once more before it had returned to the point of his
earlier danger (yet how long ago could that be counted to have
been?) And this irregular dancing backward and forward it
continued to execute for some time (yet how was that time to be
measured?) before the lord realized, as if with a new mind that
was struggling to be born within him, that its movements were
subject to his will.

He found he could determine both the speed and the direction
of the spear, have it creep toward him, even until it was only two
yards away, or fly back, have it blur in rapid interchanges of
position, have it rest at any point. Once he had demonstrated all
this, and quickened the capacities of his new mind, he sent the
weapon all the way back to his grandson, who received it in his
hand and began to rise from his crouch. Now the lord would rush
after the boy and challenge him: the odd events of the recent
past (yet how recent were they, and how past?) were instantly
forgotten in this frenzy of intention. But he found he could not.
He found himself instead turning to present his back to the
departing footsteps, then striding backward through the gallery
and hearing four rolls of thunder that gathered themselves into
gabbled sounds as his tongue touched his teeth. He turned
toward the mirror, and felt a sensation that only he in all the
world, as far as he knew, had ever felt, and that therefore he
considered inexpressible: the sensation of surprise, dismay and
puzzlement rising backward in his mind to a peak and then
suddenly vanishing as he turned his head back from the mirror
and continued his walk backward out of the gallery. He turned
himself into forward motion again and felt once more the astonishment of that glance into the mirror, then repeated the reverse
experience.

It was at that moment that he began to accept he had indeed

two minds: one that he had always known, and thought of as himself (or could one say that it thought of him as itself?), responding to events and sensations as if they were unrepeatable, and a second, just discovered in that moment of emergency, that had the power to make those events and sensations endlessly recurrent, and the ability to observe the reactions of the innocent, unwakeable first mind. And so he continued backward out of the palace, slowing himself down when it came to descending the entrance steps, though there seemed to be no hazard. He took hold of his horse again, felt the ground heave him back up into the saddle, and rode off in reverse: this again was something he at first attempted only in very decelerated motion, but he soon began to trust events to fold back as they had unfolded, and then flung himself and his mare back along the path faster than they had come (yet how much time had passed in the interim?) He got back to the cave, and to the three smaller orifices of the peri: orgasm in retrograde was disappointingly repugnant, but it could be borne, he found, for the sake of repeating the experience in forward time. So he slaked himself two hundred and eighty-two times before the distastefulness of injaculations and the boredom of his second mind overcame the insistent appetites of his first, unsated because unlearning. Then he continued on his reverse travels.

Many things on the journey delighted him. Seeing a dead bird fling itself up from the ground, trailing an arrow, then be released and fly off, albeit backward, while the arrow came back to be caught by a gathering tension in his bow: this was almost better than hunting. There was wonder too in restoring order to an overturned basket of apples, or in slicing a knife up to seal a ham, or in tracing a pen backward to pick up letters. Yet there were other things that gave him less pleasure to relive: eating backward, reversed defecation. Other sensations were, like the astonishment at the mirror, so strange as to have no vocabulary:

falling awake in the evening of a new day, or being restored to sleep in the morning, or unremembering a name before efforts to lose it, or leaping from deduction to premise.

For a long time (yet how would it have been measured?) he refused to accept the inability of his second mind to alter what had happened, or was happening, or would happen again. He returned with desperate repetition to the time when one of his daughters, at the age of three, had deeply cut her right leg with a ceremonial knife, or to the occasion when a favorite hound had rushed into the line of his arrow, or to the moment when he had told a lie to his teacher of horsemanship about a duty neglected, and his brother had uncomplainingly been whipped. Yet these events of anxiety, sadness and shame could not be altered; rather the ceaselessly unsuccessful attempts to change them increased his dread, melancholy and wretchedness, and he drew away to regions of pleasure.

Yet of course the qualities of pleasure began to decay with repetition. Because he found himself unable to alter even the minutest detail, he began to be amused, and then bored, and then appalled, and then bored again by his first mind's easy presumption that it was tasting unique sensations and making binding decisions—a presumption it never learned to unknow. He therefore came to feel increasingly that the real "he" was the second mind, that he was in his essence an observer of his first self, so that he began to feel himself detached from that self's delight, so that the excitement of existence came to reside ever more, and then only, in what he could achieve as a virtuoso of time.

Now that all sense of danger was gone, he could at will move through decades in a few seconds, while the outer world went by as flickering shadow and a low hum. Or he could make time pass so slowly that he lost track of whether it was moving forward or backward. Sometimes he wondered how he sensed time as it passed for his second mind, how he could say that decades unrolled "in a few seconds": was it merely habit, gained from the first mind? Sometimes he wondered what would happen if he were to lose this awareness of time. Would that be the loss of consciousness at last? Or would it be the gaining of a third mind, operating in time over time over time? He wished he could discuss these things with his wife, with his friends, with his counselors; but his mouth would speak only what his first mind had to say. He wondered if all those he knew, all those he met and remet, were similarly trapped into the actions and speeches of a lower consciousness; or if some were, as he had once supposed himself to be (though this was now so very long ago), innocently going through life as if time were passing once and for all; or if he were the only one to know what he supposed to be the truth.

There were, needless to say, limits to his journeyings: he could not exceed the temporal limits of his first mind. For though he could speed rapidly through the years of his adult life, in venturing back into his childhood he began to encounter resistance, so that travel through his thirteenth year began to take perhaps an hour for each month. He once invested several weeks (as he experienced them to be, and this was a long time, for his second mind never slept, though it could revisit the dreams of the sleeping first mind) in pushing back to his fifth birthday; but knowing that the forward journey would be just as arduous, he was unwilling to labor after the past any further. He felt himself to be contained in a bottle, moving freely through the fluid in the bulk of the vessel, but being slowed ever more by the thick sedimentary layers, and unable or unwilling to touch the bottom, wherever that might be. Would it be possible if he had the patience, he wondered, to push back to his birth, to reinsert himself in the womb, to witness (but from what vantage point?) the moment of his conception? And what of the time before that? But these had to remain matters for speculation.

What was more definite, or so it seemed, was the placing of

the bottle's cap. After his lengthy journey back through his childhood, he found himself spending more and more time at this other end of his life, drawing the lance ever closer, sometimes proving his command by letting it just touch his skin before making it retire, and then going back to some moment with his grandson—holding the baby in his arms, taking the boy on a fishing expedition, discussing military strategy with the adolescent—trying to alter history, which would not be altered, trying to see into the boy's mind, and then returning once more to the long gallery. There would be a time, he knew, when either by will or by error he would allow the spear to complete its journey. But not yet.

LII

in which the emperor and I
make a decision

Still we looked out on a frame of light from the Hall of Eleven Virtues. "We could sit here forever," he said, "talking and exchanging stories." "Let it be so," I said. Let it be so. Let it be so. Let the words stop.

LIII

in which someone else
hears of his return

And I heard only, as it might have been from the next cell, the insistent ring, equally regular steps, a clunk, and the voice speaking words that could not be understood, the voice that seemed to belong here with us (did we look at each other as we uncomprehendingly listened?), as if this were its true condition: to be a disembodied mumbling about us and not the malformed image of something clear beyond.

LIV

in which I meet
the marriageable maiden

⌒

~~~~~~

I watched the procession in astonishment. There were the girl servants, in white pajamas sashed with black, who entered shuffling backward, so that so many slipper soles on the bare boards made a continuous call for silence (though surely there was music), and who all bowed deeply forward from the waist, so that the eyes of each could see only the portion of floor over which the next pair of heels was shortly to follow, and so that their bodies had the form of inverted, mirrored Ls. Then there were the minor officials, in robes of cerulean silk, who were permitted an upright stance but not a forward motion, so that they stepped in slow stateliness backward; and surely there was music to give them a tempo, lest the first of them (or would they, staring through the ranks of their fellows, have felt themselves to be the last?) should inelegantly bump into the abased heads of the last (or first) of the girl servants.

And then there were those who had the good fortune to see where they were going, beginning with a group of sundry individuals who carried objects of trade or manufacture, or perhaps these were things that figured in some parade of symbols: a stocky man presented a clock on a platter of silver; a woman in emerald green bore a stuffed salamander; a scholar, for such I took him to be, had in one hand a scroll and in the other a lighted candle; a turbaned Arab gripped between both hands a glistening white china bowl edged in (I think) ultramarine; a child with untoward calm held forward a tray of oranges. And then there were grander officials, not uniform but multicolored in their robing, each carrying an ivory baton. After them came a file of waiting women, representing perhaps a lull in the crescendo of precedence; though surely there was music all the while beyond the visual. And then the climax: the princess herself, in a heavy gown of scarlet and gold continued in a train held by six eunuchs, with on her head a coronet shaped like the upper part of a fleur-de-lys, dangling with pearls and shivers of jade.

And then the music begins, or I begin to notice it: a gong is struck, and simultaneously a D-major chord sounds from muted trumpets, as if from the distance, as if in a signal. She has taken up a position close by me, while most of her attendants have proceeded past to other destinations in the place where we have congregated (but how did I get here?). It might be a palace, or a temple. There is no opportunity to make an inspection. I look into her eyes, but they are gazing slantingly past me, toward my left and beyond. I try to see if it is at all possible to turn my head so that I may see what she sees, but it is not. I am fixed. But just at the limit of my vision I can see a man behind and below us, a stick in his hand, a book before him under the glare of a lamp. It is perhaps at him that she stares, but then suddenly she switches her attention to me, and her mouth opens, the lower jaw dropping alarmingly far, the lips parting wide and tight like rubber bands around a succession of circular and elliptical objects, that succession governed by the double authority of tune and sentence, to which her chest and shoulders and inner mouthparts also move in assent, and which sets off foolish giggles in the pearls and jades of her headdress.

In questa reggia, or son mill'anni e mille . . .

She is telling me a story I know, but I also know how important is the telling, and there is something in me that does not know, or affects not to know, and that listens, knowing that it will have to respond, yet trying not to know what the response will be until the moment arrives for it to be made, endeavoring to stay in the present and shutter out the light of the future, fearing that any momentary flight into the future will be a flight from the present, introducing the terrible risk that the prescribed future will be spoiled as it comes through the crucial moment of the present on its way into the defined past. It is rare and exacting, this existence only in the present. Perhaps it will be easier when there is something to do beyond listening, watching and waiting. But there must be no "will be."

She is telling me a story of an ancestress of hers, who was abducted from here, and whose shriek of distress, though it perhaps lasted for only a few seconds many centuries ago, has been extended in her life so much longer and later. And it is me she associates with the abductor. She turns toward me with hatred in her eyes, or perhaps their message is of challenge; and as she identifies me with this defiler of her predecessor she gives me my name: "straniero." And then she turns from the story to sing of herself, and I begin to recognize in the new surge of the music something I must say, though the words have not yet arrived. I am patient. She is now looking straight ahead, at least as that direction is for her, her gaze again grazing my left shoulder. And she is building toward some moment of triumph.

Gli enigmi sono tre, la morte una!

I recognise the melody, and at once a response forms itself in my mouth; there is a sudden loss of strangeness, a moment of arrival, a wakening from a dream, or into a dream, and I find myself singing words which I can identify only in retrospect, which I seem to decipher from their echo, as if my mouth were being operated by someone else and I were merely the observer of what I achieved.

No, no! Gli enigmi sono tre, una è la vita!

And so for the first time we sing together, and then I have a moment in which to consider what these riddles may be; but I must correct myself, for to stay in the past is as dangerous as to peer into the future, and here the one entails the other. I must stay in the now, and be rewarded. Again there is a trumpet summons, but different, giving her the cue for her second call of my name, and she bids me listen to a first conundrum, which has to do with a phantom besought by everyone. I am dumbfounded, but then I am not, for the words slip my lips and give answer.

La speranza!

This is going to be easy.

LV

in which I return to the painter

But yet there must be space here for me to speak of my masters
in their quadrivium: the painter, the calligrapher, the poet and
the theologian (others were my instructors in lesser disciplines).
I will begin with the painter. Chao Meng-fu and I spoke often
of his art, whether standing before one of his works in his studio
at Taidu, or walking together through one of the city's parks, or
sharing a long dinner. He was a man of exactly my own age: he
liked to say we were two tigers at the khan's court, fierce in the
certainty and strength of our civilizations among so many who,
three generations before, were herdsmen and illiterate tent-
dwellers of the far north (not that I altogether shared his confident superiority, of course). For he was one of the rare Chinese,
and even rarer for being a noble Chinese, to occupy a post of

authority under the khan's government; though what recommended him was his artistic preeminence rather than any administrative skills, and his position as controller of architectural planning was in reality a sinecure.

His carelessness in matters of dress—his shirt might be splashed with the black-green of his pine foliage, or his trousers smeared with the sepia of his mountainsides, so that those who knew the paintings but not the painter could have recognized him by the colors of his palette—was in part a conscious affront to the contrived and borrowed elegance of the khan's court, though it also spoke of a strand of the wild in his meticulousness. Most of his paintings would remain in his studio for several years before being released as complete, and even then they might be called back, so that they could be brought up to date with the evolutions they had undergone in the painter's mind. But there were others that entered the studio as white paper and left within a few days as crowded fêtes champêtres, or group portraits, or landscapes, or animal studies, because sometimes it would happen that he could achieve his intention at once and finally, like an actor, or a man in the ecstasy of love. Sometimes he would say that only these latter paintings were really his own, since the others relied so much on what he had learned from his teachers and from the study of great masters from as far back as the Tang. At other times he would say that, on the contrary, only the former paintings were really his own, since the others were done without his intervention to steer and control. And in other moods he would hope that none of his paintings contained anything of himself, since it ought to be the aim of an artist to disappear from his work, leaving it to be created by the observer, as nature is created by the observer.

But it is as I expected: in attempting to render a portrait of Chao Meng-fu I can come up only with a disordered sequence of anecdotes and aphorisms. And yet it is hard to silence his voice now that I have set it talking.

There was this: "A painting is a landscape for the eye to wander in. It should not presume to offer a map. Still less signposts."

Or this: "There should be no viewpoints, but rather all viewpoints." This was when I tried to explain to him, inasmuch as I understood or indeed understand them, the laws by which more distant objects are painted in a picture as smaller, all in due order.

Or this: "An individual is too muddled a thing to be depicted. One paints a face in order to paint a quality, as boldness, age, nobility, graciousness, devotion." I had tried to describe what I remembered of the St. Anthony in the church of San Giovanni Battista.

Or this: "A painting is not an image of this world but a window into another. The fine duty of the artist is to present the same world as his predecessors and contemporaries, but through different windows." We were standing on a bridge between lakes, looking over to the western hills, where I had foolishly drawn attention to cloud formations which I thought resembled those in one of his landscapes.

Or this: "A painting is not in the paint but before the paint. Its life is over once it is realized."

Or this, on another occasion when we were looking toward the western hills, and I had been rash enough to propose a possible subject: "The sun sets only for the eye that sees it. A world unobserved is innocent of dusks and dawns, and it is to such a world that the viewer of a painting must think he comes, arriving first, and alone."

LVI

in which I consider
other less famed travelers

Of course there were others who came first. There were the
Franciscans, Giovanni di Piano Carpini and Guillaume de Rubrouck, who took their brown habits, their faith and their insati-
ability as far as Karakorum to treat with Kublai's predecessors
and generate material for their own books. Rubrouck's I recom-
mend to you: it is much more noticing than my own, besides
containing some excellent set pieces, like the trial of strength
with Mongu's priests, where theological debate ends quite properly with copious drinking. Nor should one forget the slightly
later account by David of Ashby, of whose book all but the
chapter headings have been lost, so that his travels may be
turned as one will, his journey a long loose thread held intermittently by pins.

And of course there were others who came later, like Ibn Battuta, touring a world of mosques and kiosks and odalisques and arabesques from Tangier to Cathay, or like those who at last conveyed books, furniture and sacraments from Rome to Peking.

And of course there were others who came at the same time, like another Franciscan, Giovanni di Montecorvino, who traveled from Europe to Peking by sea while they were on their way back (perhaps they compared notes over spiced dishes in an upper chamber in Madras), and who arrived just too late to meet Kublai, news of whose death possibly never reached Marco before his own.

And of course there were others who went in the opposite direction, like Rabban Sauma, Nestorian and native of Peking, who left while they were in the city of his birth, and who perhaps reached the city of theirs. Certainly he met two people known also to Rusticien: the pope, though by that time this office was exemplified by a different individual, Nicholas IV, and Edward Plantagenet, though by that time this individual was exemplifying a different office, king of England. It is, as they say, a small world.

LVII

in which I return to the calligrapher

He was in a turmoil of words. It seemed that scrolls were forever slithering from hooks in the ceiling down onto tables, and from there to the floor, or tumbling from cupboards, or sliding from shelves; the little room was filled with inscriptions, some consisting of just a single character on a large sheet of paper, others proposing many lines or columns, often on smaller pages, hanging on the walls in unruly clumps, or in process of descent, or blanketing the furniture, or littering the floor, like a fall of leaves.

"Our languages are, I believe," he said, "complementary. Yours is the routing of thought, like a map showing roads. Ours is the placement of ideas, like a map indicating cities. Your concern is with matters of relation, with mechanisms of connection, with means of convergence, with media of comparison, by which you link all into a single network. Our concern is with stations of identity, among which the ways may be ambiguous, tortuous, enigmatic or nonexistent.

"Our scripts, of course," he went on, "are partly responsible for these differences, for though they postdated our discoveries of speech, they have surely molded our developments of that faculty, as our gods have molded our minds. I imagine original speech as a flow of water down a smooth hillside, beginning soon to etch a riverbed—that is, a script—which will determine its course forever. You have within you broadly billowing hills, inviting streams that are sure and sound. Within us there are more precipitous escarpments, and so wandering lines of pools and waterfalls. For have you noticed that here even the land-scape speaks Chinese? It is not just the banal circumstance that we have scrawled it about with place-names; rather the shape and texture of our mountains is the shape and texture of our language. We walk within words. But come over here."

He rose from his chair, and in pushing it back knocked it into a table, which caused two or three more scrolls to complete their flow to the floor, like disturbed snakes. He came unsteadily past me, using his stick to stir papers from his path and give him some purchase on the floor, for he was already a man of great age, whom time had thinned to a crisp, wisped with thin white hair and beard. As he walked, dressed in a jacket, trousers and skullcap all of blue silk, swinging his stick before him while his left hand trailed behind, taking a long if uncertain, gingerly step, seen against a white wall of scripts, he seemed to be himself a great Tai stridden across his handiwork. I got up and followed him to the other end of his studio.

There the detritus of texts was somewhat abated. There were still scrolls hanging from the ceiling like flypapers, and the walls were still slippery with paper over paper over paper; one still felt oneself to be within a tent of calligrams. But on the table, at which he steadied himself with his right hand placed flat on its surface, there was only a single blank sheet and an oxblood papier-mâché box containing inks, brushes and seals. When I had arrived to his satisfaction, he lifted the stabilizing hand and extended it jerkily toward the box, extracting a thick brush which he dabbed into a porcelain pot of black ink. But then that hand must have been seized by some strength not its own, for it seemed that in the blink of an eye, in a single rushing flourish of inked hair on paper, a character had appeared on the page in gleaming newness.

"What do you see?" he said, as he replaced, now slowly and falteringly as before, the brush in the box, while keeping his eyes on the paper. I leafed through what I had learned of his written language.

"The character Sun," I said, and might have added, "brushed to perfection," had I not by this stage fully realized that any compliment here was regarded as otiose.

"Knowledge is not enough without understanding." His tone was more tired than dismissive.

"One translation might be 'willing submission,' " I said.

"Understanding is not enough without imagination." Again the same tone.

"A gate, leading to a house beyond, and a bare tree, or a human figure," I said after a short while, hoping that I was meeting his requirement. Suddenly I had stumbled into some kind of test.

"Imagination is not enough without perception." Again the same.

"Fresh black strokes on white paper, the ink still damp and mirroring," I said.

"Perception is not enough without insight." Yet again the same.

"A demonstration." I fear, and feared, some note of questioning could not be quite driven from my answer. How long would this go on? Not long.

"Insight is not enough without knowledge." For the last time the same.

I was silent, and after perhaps a minute, or two, or five (for I had no means of measuring time in that emptiness of thought with which he had encircled me), he turned to look up at me for the first time in these exchanges.

"Your words are as burrs: with many hooks they link together, drawn by their shared substance and common willingness to connect. Ours are as rounded pebbles: separate, individual, requiring the rotating contemplation that can never view the whole."

LVIII

in which I record the liturgy
of Buddha Christ

In die festis Inlustrationis Domini Buddhae

The Introit
The liturgical color is saffron. The celebrant approaches the altar and fans it with joss sticks.
V. Art thou he that should come, or do we look for another?
R. Seek and ye shall find. Amen.

The Ignorances
These are the seven ignorances of the bodhisattva Matthew.
I thank thee, O Father, Lord of heaven and earth, because thou hast hid these things from the wise and prudent.
No man knoweth the Son, but the Father; neither knoweth any man the Father, save the Son.

By hearing ye shall hear, and shall not understand; and seeing ye shall see, and shall not perceive.
The kingdom of heaven is like unto treasure hid in a field; the which when a man hath found, he hideth.
But he answered her not a word.
Then charged he his disciples that they should tell no man that he was Jesus the Christ.
He answered nothing.

The Buddhas
V. Christ in Buddha, *R.* Buddha in Christ, *V.* Christ in Buddha.

The Gloria Sutra
The glory of God stays hidden, else would it disturb our peace and good will. We glorify Thee for Thy strangeness, we give thanks.
V. The Lord Buddha be with you.
R. And also elsewhere.

The Collect
Grant, we beseech Thee, O God, that we may be made as mirrors to the Englightenment of Thy dear Son Lord Buddha; for the looking glass sees not and is content. Amen.

The Epistle
The Epistle is written in the sixth chapter of The Gateless Gate. When that the Lord Buddha was gone up into the mountains of Grdhrakuta, he did take up a flower, and did turn it in his fingers, and held it before his disciples. And they fell all of them silent. But one of them, who was called Maha-Kashapa, did smile at what was revealed unto him; and yet held he his face so that no man might see that he did smile. And the Lord Buddha said, Unto me is given the eye of the teaching which is true; unto me is given the heart which is of paradise. Unto me

is given the shape which hath no shape; unto me is given the step without measure which is of dharma. Nor is it to be said in words, nor in the words of my mouth, but otherwise. And behold: this teaching have I given unto Maha-Kashapa.

The Gradual
With the bodhisattva Thomas we take a hand to the hole, and feel the substance of nothing. Alleluia.

The Gospel
V. The Lord Buddha be with you.

R. And also elsewhere.

V. The Holy Gospel is written in the eighth chapter of the Gospel according to the bodhisattva John, beginning at the first verse.

R. Glory be to Thee, O Lord Buddha.

V. Jesus went unto the mount of Olives. And early in the morning he came again into the temple, and all the people came unto him; and he sat down, and taught them. And the scribes and Pharisees brought unto him a woman taken in adultery; and when they had set her in the midst, they say unto him, Master, this woman was taken in adultery, in the very act. Now Moses in the law commanded us, that such should be stoned: but what sayest thou? This they said, tempting him, that they might have to accuse him. But Jesus stooped down, and with his finger wrote on the ground, as though he heard them not.

R. Praise be to Thee, O Lord Christ.

The Creed
A period of silence may be kept.

The Offertory
V. And he suffered not the devils to speak.

R. Because they knew him.

The Canon of the Mass

V. The last supper is the only and perpetual.

R. It does not need our intervention.

The Blessing

V. The peace of God, which passeth all understanding, keep your hearts and minds unknowing. And the blessing of God Indifferent is perplexity. R. Amen.

V. Go, the Mass is endless.

R. It is indeed.

LIX

in which we come to a city
that was not there before

in which from a grille in the pavement two voices are heard in dispute as three robed figures, possibly members of the same family, their hands green with dust, walk past in a shared silence and the plan of a building blows along in the gutter, and a woman is heard speaking of a journey, or perhaps it is a man speaking of a different journey, as we pass in silence a library (the sky is cloudless blue: someone with a radio pressed to her ear and a finger to her lips is hearing the news) and a theater, and a travel agency whose promises confuse, where again we hear the underground voices (we must have come full circle) until they are further submerged by that of a young man talking excitedly into a public telephone, close by which we buy a newspaper from a street vendor, while a young woman with a face of intent stops for a moment and continues, and we walk on in the opposite direction past the law courts, where other disputations might meet our ears, and we stop to open the color supplement, leaning on a wall by the hospital (a taxi passes: there is a shock of recognizing a familiar face out of context, but no, it cannot be), and we walk on, treading grime into an abandoned photograph as we pass the casino and an electrical shop inside which a telephone is ringing while the proprietor sleeps, which makes us remember something of no importance, so that we miss noticing the priest who strides past with his arm over a fat yellow book, and only return to attention when a hole opens at our feet, causing us to stop and look back at the priest, then step carefully around the building works, brushing past two strangers in solemn conversation (a radio calls operatically from an upper story) and turning west into the sunset, overhearing rumors, ignoring a poster that flaps in the evening wind, striding past the cathedral, going on

LX

in which someone tells
of the last of five visits
to places of interest in Peking

There must have been a first time that we were walking side by
side along the path through the forest, between the banks where
the rusted bracken of the previous season, stiff and broken, was
beginning to topple under pressure from tightly curled new
fronds, and where the white stars of wood anemones were beginning to open, and where the air around us was skimmed with
a first mist of insects, and where he said: "This may be something to interest you." For we had turned a corner in the path
and had before us the prospect of a timber teahouse, which on
the side facing us boasted a veranda and, in front of that, a
railed-off court. Groups of two and three and four were lying on
the ground within the court, or standing in conversation on the
veranda or on the steps that led up to it, or seated at windows

within the teahouse. Other lone figures on the scene carried trays into or out from the building: it was a panorama of the utmost civility and liveliness.

"Many come here," said the Failed Sage as we went through the central gap in the fence allowing entrance to the court and thence to the teahouse, "merely for the entertainment of an outing, but we are honored to have been granted an audience with the tea-master himself. First, however, we may take refreshment with the others." We had by now reached the steps up to the veranda, and I was surprised by the quietness. For though the great throng of people suggested a holiday, all that could be heard was the occasional distant chink of a porcelain cup in a porcelain saucer, or the nearer, much less localized murmur of subdued conversation, or the nearer still, and now again quite definable, creak of wood as I placed a foot on the first step. We continued up, entered the teahouse, and found a table in the interior gloom.

The impression, once one was inside, was of a much larger building than it had seemed: there was room for perhaps thirty tables, each of which could have seated eight without discomfort, and which were well separated from one another. At one of them, over to my right, way beyond my companion (who was leaning forward to read some paper), were two people twisted in their chairs to stare out through the window, he in a red tunic, she in a blue coat: theirs would have been the two unsmiling faces I had noticed as we approached the teahouse, and I drew confidence from their presence that there was indeed a necessary connection between the sunny, airy exterior and this present dark, where the atmosphere was stale with an excess of being breathed, and stale too with the memories of an earlier week's spices.

But the paper he was reading was probably not a menu, because while he still read a young woman came tottering dangerously toward us, curving a line through the spaces between tables, with a tray of tea: a pot, two bowls, and a plate of what at first I took to be seashells, though a delighted second examination identified them as sweetmeats of painted sugar and marzipan. We nibbled at these and sipped our tea, and said nothing. His eyes were still fastened on the crumpled sheet of paper, which he would turn in order to inspect the reverse side, and then after a minute or so turn again. Mine, now that they had grown accustomed to the dimness, were free to range over the other occupants, most of whom, unlike us, were sitting at windows and looking out. Then, quite suddenly, at no signal, as if perhaps the action itself were the signal, he folded the paper into his right sleeve and stood.

"It is time for us to visit the tea-master," he said, and began to walk toward the doors through which the bobbing waitress had brought us our teas. I took another gulp from my bowl and rose to follow the bulky shape of ultramarine moving among the tables, which now appeared rather more closely packed.

The doors gave entrance not, as I had expected, to a kitchen but to a corridor, leading straight ahead and having three doors on each side, as well as a seventh at the end. Doors, floors, walls and ceiling were all of unvarnished wood, and all disappeared when the doors back to the tearoom swung behind me, for there was no window or other means by which light might have found its way into this far recess of the teahouse. However, the shuffle of my companion's slippers enabled me to follow him to the middle door on the right, and when this was opened light was restored, for an oil lamp burned on a low table, revealing to me (though no doubt not to him, who would have needed no revelation) that we had entered a cubicle of perhaps nine feet in each dimension. Again the construction was entirely of wood, and again there was no window, nor any furniture or decoration except for the table and the lamp, nor any personages except for ourselves and the tea-master, who sat on the floor behind the table, looking into the flame. He had long mustaches but no beard, and his head was bare. He sat with his legs folded beneath him and a hand on each knee, his robes falling in deep pleats from his shoulders, arms and knees: their colors could not be named, for they reflected only the orange-brown suffusion of the lamp. He was perfectly still.

Following my companion's example, I sat on the floor in an attitude approximating to that of the tea-master, assuming that this was indeed he. In the silence it seemed an intrusion to look at him, even though our reason for being there was to see him, and even though there was nothing else on which to fix one's eyes, unless the lamp. But I had time in which to overcome my embarrassment. I looked for some movement in his eyes, but there was none. I looked for some undulation of his garments in response to his respiration, but again there was none. Then, in an instant of passage from clouded confusion to banal certainty, it occurred to me that we had been admitted to the presence of a statue, and I looked at the tea-master, or perhaps I should now say "purported tea-master," with a newly freed, rivetted attention. If a statue, was he made of wood, or stone, or bronze, or ceramic? Wood seemed the most likely, in company with all the wood around him: no other material, surely, could have given him such a warm, absorbent texture. And yet the carving of the mustaches, still unmoving, would have to have been the work of a master; and since no join could be seen in the figure—no, not even in the belting of the waist—he must have been eased from the trunk of a remarkably large tree: a great fig, perhaps, such as I had seen in the old imperial gardens of Hangchow.

And the more I stared, the more I became convinced that he was indeed a work of nature in his substance but of man in his shape. I began to accumulate evidence: the drapery on his right arm (I could not see the left) was not quite convincing in its fall, and near the right knee there was a spot that looked very like a knot, and, yes, on the chest were there not five cracks such as the drying heat of the lamp might over years or decades or centuries have opened? But I was unable to continue my examination of these diagnostic features, because my companion rose without warning, and without taking his leave made toward the door. I went after him, and we had left the corridor and the teahouse and the courtyard, were back on the path through the forest before a word was spoken.

"Did the tea-master answer your question?" my companion then asked.

This question of his at once blotted out my suspicions, even though they had become convictions, and I stupidly felt a pang of regret that I had been in the presence of an oracle and failed to make use of it, when in all likelihood there would not be a second chance, as indeed there was not.

"But I asked no question!" I said.

"It is as you say. However, the greatest questions are never asked, and I had thought you were wondering whether the tea-master was a living being or a statue."

There were to be, or had already been, so many instances of my failure to take account of his subtlety. "Indeed I was," I said. "Can you enlighten me?"

"That may take longer than you suppose, for the greatest answers are never given." We continued walking in silence for perhaps a minute or two. "However, there are lower levels where discourse is possible, and perhaps I may tell you something of the tea-master, whom of course we call the tea-master merely because he has his dwelling in the teahouse."

"I should be grateful," I said, "for any information."

"Information, alas, is not mine to vouchsafe: I have not, as you know, attained that eminence. But I may tell you a story."

LXI

in which the Failed Sage
tells a story

"The tea-master, whom we call also the breaker of categories, is charged with responsibility for eroding old distinctions in the world by introducing new ones. According to one version of the story, he was present when the universe began in the distinction of all from nothing. Before that period, of course, if we may speak of a time before time, all was nothing and nothing was all: the moment of distinction was the moment of origin. However, some argue that since the only things in the universe at that moment of origin were all and nothing, then the tea-master cannot have been there at all, since he would have constituted a third thing. Others hold that he is not a thing but a person, which is quite a different matter, and that not only was he there when all first separated itself from nothing and nothing from all, but that he was there before, always allowing that we may speak of a time before time. There is also a third school of thought, according to which the dissociation of all from nothing was simultaneous with the dissociation of tea-master from non-tea-master, and that these two dissociations—of matter from non-matter and of person from non-person—were inextricably and inevitably interdependent. However, these academic disputes are perhaps—"

"Wait," I said. "If the tea-master is a statue, then he could hardly have existed when there was no matter."

"As a statue indeed. But perhaps a statue is a representation of a person, even as this body walking beside me is a representation of you. If I touch your arm," and he did so, "do I touch you, or do I merely touch your arm? Surely I can never touch the you that is a breath within your mind."

"No, but I know my mind began with the birth of my body."

"Is it in your mind that the sun warms?" "Yes," I said. "That food and water are necessary to life?" "Yes," I said again. "Then in those respects your mind is congruent with those of the lizard and the tree. You are perhaps not so young as you imagine."

I think I knew even at this stage that there would be no point in insisting that my sense of myself depended not on these generalities but on tastes and opinions and, most especially, memories that I shared with no other being, for he would surely have said, as surely he did say at some other time, that my sense of myself is a very different thing from myself. In any event, he was already continuing the story.

"Accounts differ as to which categories were next broken by the tea-master in his efforts to redress the easy sovereignty of all and nothing, though most agree that the next separation was between dark and light, and many maintain that the third distinction was between solid and liquid, and not a few share the view that the fourth division was between living and non-living. Thereafter the possibilities ramify beyond the time we have at our disposal, the further divisions affecting the universe in increasingly partial respects. The parting between bony and cartilaginous, for instance, affected the category of fishes, but not that of stars, or jokes, or rainbows. And so the breaker of categories continued his work until the universe had become as we know it."

"And is his work now complete?"

"The nature of your question and the fact of your asking it require the answer 'yes,' for how could we live and converse in a world still growing? But again there are diverse hypotheses. Some say that the universe has now achieved stability because the breaker of categories is dead. Others would wish to retain the possibility that his work continues, but in such fine distinctions that we cannot detect them. Still others ask us to live in constant expectation of some new cataclysm."

LXII

in which I meet the famed traveler nearer at hand

For there might be the trekking not only through desert and plain and mountain pass and city street and desiccated riverbed, not only through page and paragraph, but through square silent corridors, and empty halls, through bequests and benefactions and plunders and purchases as:

Item. A stemmed cup of Qingbai ware of the Yüan dynasty, the hemispherical bowl hexagonally fluted so that it has the appearance of a flower, the whole translucent white except where the material is thicker and grays the light. It is one of a pair he gave to the concubine on her wedding. The other was broken soon afterward, under circumstances that have not been recorded, but from this one they would, on summer afternoons, alternately sip at cooled infusions of mint, or poppy petals, or pine needles, or honey and sandalwood, or star anise. And later, when they were at sea, he found the princess had brought it with her, more as a memento than as a part of her dowry, carrying it half way westward and leaving the completion of the journey for the next six centuries to accomplish, as wavelets will hesitantly but inexorably complete the stranding of an object borne near the shore in the foam of a breaker.

Item. An enameled glass mosque lamp, made to hold perhaps a gallon of oil, shaped like a fat thistle head, with texts shouted in blue over the neck and in transparent strokes on a blue ground around the belly, and with other decoration of red tracery and little flowers. It is said to have been made for the Mamluk sultan Muhammad ibn Qala'un (1294–1340), but he saw it being carried as a prize with much ceremony into the church of St. George at Trebizond on the return journey, flame spilling onto the sand of the street, over the dalmatics of six bare-footed deacons, and upon the quivering outstretched arms of suppliants.

Item. A bowl in alkaline-glazed frit ware from northern Iran, glistening white and edged in dark blue, with below that edge a border of translucent spots, and inside, at the bottom, a scrawl which the catalogue reports to represent a duck beneath a tree, though it might as well be merely a smudging of paint, or a monogram, or a character in some unknown script. The same authority dates it with appealing modesty to "c.1250–1300," though we are able to give a more precise terminus ante quem, since he saw it filled with fresh figs on a table beside the divan of a courtesan in Tun at 7:48 P.M. on August 12, 1272.

Item. A Longquam celadon bowl, gray-green, with a pair of goldfish modeled in the bottom. And molded into it with the same firmness of purpose, in his thoughts, are the stubby fingers of the emperor himself, trawling for cashews within a salad of nuts as they spoke of the Holy Trinity.

Item. A rather more than lifesize figure of the bodhisattva Avalokitesvara, seated on a dais, with his right hand raised and his left invisibly, because it has been lost, resting on his left knee. Elaborate draperies fall from his shoulders, across his chest and from around his waist; a large bow also hangs down lankly between his outstretched legs, suggesting an immense fecundity disdaining action. On his head there is a coronet of floral fantasy, woven about his intricately plaited hair; and he wears a jewel in his forehead. He is designed to impose from the front: the sides and the rough back are hewn with box-shaped cavities, by means of which he might have been attached to some altar or carried in procession. Apart from the single hand, which may well be a later replacement, he would appear to contain no join, and so to have been carved from the trunk of a remarkably large tree (from a fig, we are told), and then covered with gesso and color, of which some survives in traces of crimson and cobalt on the clothing, pink on the large oval ears, and black on the hair. The description has it that he was made in Shanxi around 1300, but that is not quite correct, for our informant saw him emerging, like a grand, male, severe, sedentary Daphne in reverse, during the summer of 1287 in the Peking workshop of Master Chu Kia-fu, who was also responsible for the doorposts of the Hall of Eleven Virtues. There was a foolish tradition in the eighteenth century, which possibly came to the ears of Coleridge, that this figure preserves a likeness of the great khan; but of course this is a Chinese and not a Mongol face, besides which Master Chu was not in the habit of copying from life, though we should add that our informant has reported a similarity between these unknowing, near-closed eyes and those of a companion who was his guide.

LXIII

in which I return to the poet

Two years later he would place a dream of three worlds they had not dreamt, of rivers and cliffs and steps and angels and ice sheets beyond their style. Can one imagine him turning the pages of what someone with less scruple about anachronism might call the "best seller" of his day? Can one imagine him visiting, if only in imagination, the cell where they caught each other's thoughts as swiftly as a mirror catches appearances?

Five hundred years later he would record another dream, but say it was only a part of what he had dreamt under the influence of his "anodyne."

Six hundred and eighty-nine years later both the entirety and the fragment would elude him.

LXIV

in which he returns
to the place of origin

The first impression above the rooftops was of a gondola, but
without any balloon to support it up there: just a great white
straight-sided bowl of people a hundred and fifty feet up in the
air, askew to normality, tilted toward him, most of the floaters
nevertheless fearlessly leaning over, pointing toward features on
the ground, talking excitedly, audible even at this distance. But
there was no balloon; and the gondola did not move; and its sides
were not of basketwork or canvas but of shining marble. And
it was seeing that fact of the stoniness that made him see what
it was that he was seeing, the two recognitions of substance and
form coming instantaneously, and instantaneous with them the
pleasure and relief that he had succeeded in his aim of coming
upon one of the most celebrated of buildings unawares, nude as

a child. For he had taken only the barest glance at a map displayed at the railway station, gleaning more the direction than the route. He knew this to be a sort of homecoming. It might be important.

Much of the book, after all, was already prepared, if only in outline, if only as a run of chapter headings. Of course there was the fact of the two men in the cell: he had visited the birthplace of the first in his teens, and then again in the autumn of 1984, superstitiously touching stones that he might have touched, by canals he might have scanned; now it was the turn of the other on this June 29, 1986, the feast of SS. Peter and Paul, halfly his name day. At some point between these dates, between these cities, had come the decision that there should be sixty-four chapters based on the hexagrams of the I Ching, in their conventional order and with their conventional attributes. He would also have known by now that he would be leaning on the original book, in Ronald Latham's translation for Penguin, a well-traveled companion. No doubt there would be something too out of Liu Jung-en's *Six Yüan Plays* (Penguin, 1972), volumes III and IV of *Lands and Peoples: The World in Color* (Grolier Society, 1932–57), Fung Yu-lan's *A Short History of Chinese Philosophy* (Macmillan, 1960), Réne Kappler's edition of Rubrouck's *Voyage dans l'empire mongol* (Payot, 1985), Lee Shiu Keung's *The Cross and the Lotus* (Christian Study Centre on Chinese Religion and Culture, 1971), Paul Reps's *Zen Flesh, Zen Bones* (Penguin, 1971), Liu Junwen's *Beijing: China's Ancient and Modern Capital* (Foreign Language Press, Beijing, 1982), a yet unpublished telephone directory and so much else. Somehow these things would have to be acknowledged.

And so would those other books of the dead: the museums. There was that large picture of exactly the right period in the Metropolitan, with its tantalizing view of an older man sitting on a donkey led by a servant, while a younger man follows on booted foot, the three of them wholly dominated by a pine tree that is a huge complex character, itching with meaning to the tips of its many bare twisted branches, to the points of the few needles that still cling after so many winters. Perhaps he still felt that this would have to find a place, not yet knowing that he would find material nearer at hand, in the Ashmolean, not knowing that as he sat drinking a cup of coffee at an outdoor café, perusing the three buildings laid out before him like an exhibition of geometrical solids: the baptistery a raised hemisphere, the cathedral a nonagonal prism, the campanile a pure cylinder, in intention. Or they might have been the guises of mosque, court and minaret, or temple, hall and pagoda. He reached into his pocket for a cigarette.

And before that he had been into the Duomo, seen Dante's emperor suspended in effigy in the south transept, and heard the great length of the reverberations of chants and summonses, trying to distinguish when a sound died away completely, but unable to because the moment of completion never came, so that he concluded that what was sung and spoken here never did fall into silence but only grew steadily weaker from echoing to echoing, and would continue to grow steadily weaker even through centuries, never quite vanishing, so that he could fold his voice into his and say, under cover of a prayer, almost as a prayer: "*Buon giorno,* Rustichello."

LXV

in which another book continues
after the present one is over

~~~~~~

Or avint que a les MCLXXXVII anz de l'ancarnasion de Crist
les Tartars font un lor roi avoit a nom en lor lengajes Cinghis
Can. Cestui fui home de grant valor et de gran senz et de grant
proesse . . .